HURRY HOME CANDY

by Meindert DeJong

Pictures by Maurice Sendak

FONTANA : LIONS

First published in 1953 by Harper & Brothers, New York
First published in Great Britain 1962 by Lutterworth Press
First published in Fontana Lions 1977
by William Collins Sons & Co. Ltd
14 St James's Place, London SW1

Text © Meindert DeJong 1953

Printed in Great Britain
by William Collins Sons & Co. Ltd, Glasgow

This is the story of a small dog's search for a home. Once he had been loved, and had a home, as the pet of two young children – though there were times of loneliness and fear, and the terror of their mother's broom whenever he did something wrong.

Then one day, on a trip to the country, there was a storm, the car broke down, and in the confusion Candy was left behind. He became a stray, terrified of human beings, scared of other dogs, and only driven to visit houses round about at night because of the hunger which gnawed at him. Through his many adventures, with the pig woman on her wagon, the policeman, George the kindly keeper of the dogs' home, and the captain, he gradually comes to find trust and affection once more.

Meindert DeJong holds the National Book Award of America, the Newbery Medal and the Hans Christian Andersen Medal for his lasting contribution to children's literature. Maurice Sendak, who has illustrated *Hurry Home Candy*, was awarded the Hans Christian Andersen Illustrator's Medal.

Other titles in Lions

The Search for Delicious *Natalie Babbitt*
Little Lord Fauntleroy *Frances Hodgson Burnett*
Journey from Peppermint Street *Meindert DeJong*
Along Came a Dog *Meindert DeJong*
The Donkey Rustlers *Gerald Durrell*
The New Noah *Gerald Durrell*
The Talking Parcel *Gerald Durrell*
The Phantom Tollbooth *Norton Juster*
The Demon Bike Rider *Robert Leeson*
The Last Bus *William Mayne*
Mind Your Own Business *Michael Rosen*
The Rescuers *Margery Sharp*
and five other 'Miss Bianca' stories

and many more

For ELIZABETH NOWELL

and poets of her ilk

CONTENTS

PART ONE: THE MEMORY

I.	The Dog	9
II.	The Two Old People	12
III.	The Memory of Fear	18
IV.	The Broom	26
V.	The Ride	34
VI.	The Bridge	44
VII.	The Night	54
VIII.	The Stray Year	62

PART TWO: THE WAY HOME

IX.	The Chicken	65
X.	The Wagon	72
XI.	The Handbag	81
XII.	The Dogs' Home	91
XIII.	The Children's Ward	99
XIV.	The Captain	106
XV.	The Heavenly Week	113
XVI.	The Hike	123
XVII.	Candy or Jinx	132
XVIII.	The Wound	139
XIX.	Hurry Home, Candy	148

PART ONE

THE MEMORY

1. THE DOG

The dog had no name. For a dog to have a name someone must have him and someone must love him, and a dog must have someone. The dog had no one, and no one had the dog. The dog had only the silent empty countryside of the few houses. The dog had only the crumbs and cleaned bones he could pick up at the few houses. The dog had only himself, so the dog had nothing, and he was afraid.

He was a scared little whip-tailed cur. He was a stray, and he seemed to have been born a stray. He clung to a small area of countryside just a few miles outside a town. In a furtive, hidden, almost wild-animal way he had made it his own. Here the houses were few, and where houses are few, people are few, and he was afraid. He was afraid of people.

But even though the people were few, the dog kept himself to the back fields, the copses, the fences and hedgerows, the shadows. The copses were shadowy and dark – hiding places, lurking places where the dog could live unseen. The fences and hedgerows were weedy and thorny and deep – secret travelling avenues along which the dog could move about unnoticed and unseen by the people and the other dogs of the countryside.

Hunger drove the dog to the few scattered houses of the people, but only at night. At night – well after midnight – when all light and life were gone from the houses, he made his rounds. He knew every house.

He knew the houses where the watch-dogs lived, and he knew the houses where there were no dogs. He knew the houses where at night the dogs were kept locked up to bark uselessly at him when he made his stealthy darkness rounds. He knew the dogs of that whole countryside, but saw to it that they knew him only as a scent and a stealthy movement round about their houses in the night. But much more important to the all-important knowledge of his nightly meagre sources of food, the little dog knew the houses where the women shook out the table-cloths outdoors. He knew at which houses the women set out too much food for the early-roosting chickens. He scoured up the crumbs; he finished off the pecked-over chicken food; he dug up the buried bones of the dogs so that he might live another night.

Hunger haunted the dog. It sat like an agony behind his eyes. Hunger ached out of his ladder-rung ribs, those lean ribs that threatened to break through the stretched, shivering skin. Always the dog shivered. When at rest he shivered. Not from cold necessarily, but from hunger, from fear, from loneliness, and from lovelessness – mostly, perhaps, from lovelessness, for the dog had nothing but himself.

Sometimes the haunting hunger drove the little dog out of his copse hiding places by day. But only when hunger became bigger than fear. Only on days when he had not been able to find a dead rabbit or crow, or hadn't been able to catch a quick, scurrying field mouse. On such days he would emerge from his shadowy copse. By secret avenues of hedgerow and fence he would whip himself across the furtive fields to still another copse. In the hope of finding something dead there, or of catching a mouse there. In that hope.

And sometimes on those furtive trips from copse

to copse he was seen. A woman looking out of a

window might see a distant flash of something brown
and white, but it would be little more than a streak and
a shadow going into the shadows. Sometimes a man
working in a field would catch a movement from
the corner of his eye, but the flash and the shadow
would be gone even as the man jerked his eyes around
to search it out. That was all the dog was to anyone
in that countryside – a flash and a shadow gone into
the shadows. It wasn't a particular dog that they had
seen before; it was just the shadowy movement of
what they supposed to be a dog. No one in that
countryside really knew the dog existed. No one was
sure. Still the dog had lived there for a year.

But now in the last two weeks of his stray year
the little dog had added a house on another road to his
nightly rounds. A house where two old people lived

with a toothless, rheumatic old hound. The hound was too toothless to gnaw bones, too old and weary with life to bury his bones. But still the old hound obeyed his dog instincts and shoved his bones under an old sack against the wall of a shed where he lay during the day sunning his rheumatic joints. And the little dog knew.

Now in the last week the dying old hound had even become too weary with life to eat the pan of mushy meat and vegetables set out for him every evening. And the little dog knew. Oh, how he knew, for because of the toothless old hound, the little dog had not gone hungry for a week. It was the first time in his year-long stray life. The house of the two old people became his first stop on his nightly rounds of the dark houses of the countryside. And that was how two old people became aware of the little dog's existence. Two old people – just beginning to suspect that the stray dog existed. It all came about because of the toothless old hound, and a picture window.

2. THE TWO OLD PEOPLE

The dog sat shivering in the maple tree copse at the back of the farm of the two old people and the toothless hound. The late afternoon sun trekking towards the horizon sent its warmth under the branches of the maple trees, but the dog shivered. Stared and shivered. Suddenly he raised his head and a strange thin cry issued out of his throat. It rose sharp and eerie, it whined away over the fields. It frightened the dog, scared him into snapping his jaws shut. He sat and stared.

It was the same queer cry that had come out of him last night when he had sat on the freshly dug grave of the toothless old hound. The old hound had died and had been buried, and as the little dog had sat forlorn on the turned-up earth of the grave, the hopeless whining cry had come rising up out of him. It had gone on and on. Not for any love of the old hound, but from deep loneliness and hunger. There had been no bones under the sack, and no mush in the white enamelled pan.

Last night, too, his own lost wail had scared and surprised the little dog. It had betrayed him. Light had snapped on in the house. He had shrunk back into the shadows of a shed. He had slunk to his copse. After betraying himself with his helpless whining he had not dared to make the rounds of the other houses that night.

Now here it was again, the thin, lost, haunted cry coming out of him in broad daylight. It would betray him, give away his whereabouts. The dog sat still; even his eyes did not move. He stared straight ahead through the brush at the old farmer in the back field. The old man had heard him, he had stopped his horses; now he stooped, trying to penetrate the brush and shadows in the copse. The dog sat still, not even moving his eyes.

The troubled farmer straightened up, stood a while, his eyes roving uneasily along the copse, but then he clucked to his horses. At last the clank and clink of the jogging harnesses was gone. The man and his horses were gone. Only the heavy sweat odours of the horses still lingered like something damp and heady in the warm, late sunshine. Suddenly the dog moved, ran furtively, swiftly from shadow to shadow on his long way to another, safer copse to hide there and wait there until his crumb night came.

He had to cross a bare space in a field. Stretched low, hunched small, whip-fast, he hurtled himself across the space, lost himself in one flowing motion among the tall rows of a blackberry patch. He ran more upright then along the sheltering rows of black-berries. He rushed on to his new hide-out.

At the house of the dead, toothless hound, the old woman sat sewing at a big picture window that held the whole countryside of fields and trees and the rise and roll of the hills in its ample frame. Now as she glanced up her eye caught the momentary flash of the dog over the bare spot in the field. He melted into the shadows of the blackberry patch. The old woman sat staring at the spot where the dog had been. She was troubled.

In full daylight she glanced a little fearfully behind

her into the room. It was as if she had heard the clicking of dog feet on the linoleum behind her in the hall.
'But old Butch is dead,' she reminded herself anxiously
in the quiet house. 'He's dead and buried.' She shivered.

Her eyes roved back to the picture window. She
mumbled to herself, thinking troubled thoughts. If she
hadn't bought the big window – it could have been
smaller – it had been so costly, too, having it installed.
If she had listened to her husband, instead of spending
all that money on the window. That's what he'd said :
'Let's get another dog right away to take old Butch's
place when he dies. That way it won't hurt so much.'

She ran her eyes over the window again. It was
funny how buying the window had come back to haunt
her. The week the window had been installed had also
been old Butch's last week. Old Butch should really
have been at the vet's that week. But she'd begrudged
the old hound that last comfort. She had to have
the window installed so there wouldn't be any pos-
sibility, if Butch died, of getting her to use part of
the money for a new dog. Those, if she was honest, had
been her thoughts ! It seemed mean now. She shook her
head over herself in shamed astonishment.

Her eyes shot to the spot in the field in front of
the blackberry patch. The bare sunlit spot in the field
lay empty.

It was funny how the window had come to plague
her. It wasn't until she'd got the big window that she'd
seen it – that shadow of a swift dog shape, that flash
of brown and white, seen and gone. Swift, where old
Butch was slow and rheumatic, almost like the swift
ghost of old Butch – even the same colour Butch had
been – brown and white.

Now she'd seen it again. And then last night, that
awful cry coming out of the yard, right from the spot

where Butch had been buried. It had jerked her straight up in bed, and before her husband had snapped on the light she'd plainly seen the fresh-turned black dirt, and then a dog shadow shrinking away. Her husband had heard the haunted crying, too, and they'd both lain awake and troubled. Nonsense, of course, superstitious nonsense! But wasn't it strange? She'd never seen the flash of the shadowy dog before, she'd never heard the haunted lost cry before – until after Butch had died.

The door opening on its dry hinges startled her. She whirled to face it. It was her husband. 'Well?' she said defiantly to hide her shakiness. 'Well, aren't you quitting early?' she tried to say normally.

'I finished ploughing the back field,' he said reasonably. 'Do you know, Martha, I heard it again on the back forty acres – coming out of our maple copse – that same crazy queer cry as last night. Not a dog's and still a dog's. It bothered me, and I could have sworn a pair of eyes were staring at me out of the copse. But, oh, broad daylight – I shook it off. It's been bothering me ever since though.'

He just baldly came out with it – men didn't hide things. 'I saw it again, too,' she admitted now. 'That flash and shadow that I've been telling you about. Like a dog, but not enough at least to make sure.' Then she blurted it out. 'Like the ghost of a dog. And it looks like Butch – brown and white. It had me shivering.'

Her husband uttered a queer short cackle of a laugh. 'I told you we should have got another dog. But you had to have that picture window! And now you see ghosts through it. But that's what comes when you get old. I catch myself all the time in the barn turning around, thinking it's Butch, sort of seeing him. How you miss him then!'

'Me, too. I hear him come clicking over the linoleum. I wish we'd taken Butch to the vet's his last week, and I wish we hadn't buried him beside the shed.'

'Oh, come now,' her husband said. 'What we hear and see is most likely some stray dog skulking around the place. Wish we could lure him to the house. He'd be better than nothing, better than ghost thoughts, anyway. Ghost of a dog!' He cackled his harsh troubled laugh. 'You certainly start seeing things when you get old,' he derided himself, and her.

The thought of luring the stray to the house appealed to her. 'I'll set out a pan of food for him tonight,' she announced.

'Yes, do that,' her husband said.

When her husband had gone to the barn for the evening chores she set out Butch's white enamelled pan with some hashed meat and vegetables. Having done that she fetched a washing-up bowl of water which she sprinkled all around the pan with the dog food. With a broom she swept the sopped mud into flat smoothness. 'Well, if it's a dog, it'll leave tracks when it goes after the food,' she explained her trick to herself. 'And if it isn't . . .' She stood still. If it were a ghost it wouldn't need food and wouldn't leave tracks. But any loose dog that passed would gulp the food, she reminded herself, and there'd be plenty of tracks in the morning.

Then she got honest with herself, and admitted that the test really was that the food would be gone, but there wouldn't be a single track in the sopped mud around the pan. That was what was at the bottom of her mind. She shivered.

The clanking of the milk pails indicated that her husband was coming from the barn. 'Two old fools,' she whispered. But she waited for him just inside the door, did not venture by herself into the shadowy, hollow house.

3. THE MEMORY OF FEAR

The little dog sat shivering in the copse. A night wind was sighing among the pines. This was the pine copse, another copse on poorer soil where pines grew and a sand creek flowed. The creek rustled in the night. The hide-out of the dog was far from the maple copse of the two old people; too far for the little dog's hunger-sharpened nose to pick up the smell of the hashed meat and vegetables set out for him by the old woman.

He wouldn't have gone even had he smelled the food. He wouldn't have dared; didn't dare now to make his nightly rounds of the houses in the countryside. He was afraid of betraying himself by his whining. In his life of fear stood a new fear – the fear of betraying himself.

Under the deep-branched pines the little dog sat sorrowing.

It was over. The old dog was dead. The enamelled food pan had been cleaned. His brief happiness, the brief security of regular food was over.

Miserably out of his stretched throat rose the thin, piercing whine. It sang about his head under the low-boughed pines. It went on and on, unloved and empty. He could not stop it.

The old life of hunger and loneliness and fear was back. He had nothing but himself and a memory.

The little dog's memory began in fear. In that memory he had not been born a stray, had not always been a stray, but almost immediately his fear and frightened bewilderment had begun. It began as of that cold moment when hands lifted him out of the warm nest where with his puppy brothers he was snuggled against the great warm milk-giving body of his mother.

This time the hands that lifted him did not replace him in the nest as always before. Already in his dim puppy sight he was miles away from his mother and his puppy nest, the moment he was lifted. He stayed in the air, in the hands. He was carried away. Excited voices were right above him. The faint warm odour of his mother left him. Next the smell of the house in which he had been born went away. He was outdoors in cold, stinging air.

He was being carried along a street. Thunderous noises clapped against his ears from everywhere. Those noises were all around him; above him there was the constant, excited chatter of the little boy who was carrying him, and of the little girl who was walking tightly against her brother to be as close to the puppy as possible.

The little dog was bringing excited happiness to the two children. They had bought him, now they were carrying him home. Now he was their dog. The puppy, of course, understood none of this. The puppy only understood in a confused way the goneness of the warm, secure mother and the nest. The sharpness and coldness of the outside air hit him where the boy's arm did not shelter him. But somehow, little as he was, the puppy dimly sensed the love and excitement in the two voices above him. He somehow knew that he was being loved in a new way.

It was only when the boy and girl, playfully experimenting with their treasure, set him down, that the sharpness of the loss of nest and mother pierced into the puppy's heart. There he stood splay-legged, staring up in bewildered milky-eyed near-sightedness at the two white faces far above him. Desperately he whimpered up at the faces, as he stood shivering in the great strange world on a cold, hard slab of sidewalk. 'Ah, poor little thing, he's so cold,' the girl said. She scooped him up and cradled him in soft warm arms. 'It's my turn now,' she told her brother. 'He's mine, too, you know.'

Then there was another house. No mother, no brothers, no sisters were in this house. No nest. No furry warmth to snuggle into, snuggle and drink, crawl under and into, deeper and warmer, to sleep and drink warm milk. No nest in which to wrestle with another soft puppy with fierce puppy growls, only in the midst of the battle to forget and fall asleep or burrow under for another drink. Another house – a cold house, cold-clean house with hard clean smells; no mother, sister, brother smells.

There were new voices. The heavier voices of a man and woman in among the excited shrill voices of the little boy and girl. He was set down on the kitchen linoleum. There he stood. His splayed-out puppy legs slipped farther apart on the cold, slippery, waxed linoleum. He slid, legs in every direction, down into a clumsy little puppy heap.

He looked up from his helpless little heap, and all the voices above roared as one great roar. The laughter roared until the laughter shrieked. Suddenly he was terribly afraid. 'Watch him!' the woman screamed. All the laughter stopped. The puppy was jerked up from the floor by the scruff of his neck. He felt himself dangling, sailing. A door opened, and he was dropped. The door banged shut. He was all alone in the cold outdoors. He had landed too hard. He sat whining softly where he had landed, understanding none of it.

The door opened, the little girl was picking him up, cuddling him in her soft warm arms. Her face nuzzled his woolly fur. 'You didn't know, did you? You don't know about houses yet.'

She carried him back into the kitchen. He felt a little more secure because it was warm in her arms. Suddenly the woman's big white face loomed close. The puppy looked up at her. 'Not even house trained,' the woman said harshly near the puppy's ear. 'This isn't going to be a joke!'

'Oh, we'll take care of it, Mother,' the girl promised anxiously. 'We'll watch him and train him . . .'

The woman made snorting noises. 'Yes, yes, I know those promises – good for a day or so, and then it'll be up to me. Believe me, he's going to learn fast, I'll see to that . . . But he is a sweet little thing,' she said more calmly. Her face came closer still. The puppy shrank back against the girl.

The man's big round face was thrust beside the woman's. 'Nicely marked,' the man said. 'But it doesn't look to me as if he's got much spirit. Some dogs start out feeling whipped, you know.' His face stayed there. 'House-trained, hah!' his voice exploded. 'Looks to me as if he mightn't even be weaned yet. You kids got him too soon. I suppose you couldn't wait, but it would be a mercy if you took him back to his mother for another week . . . I doubt if he can even drink out of a saucer.'

The puppy was lowered to the floor. He was placed before a saucer of cold milk.

He sprawled before the saucer, his weak little legs started slipping. He didn't even see the white milk in the white saucer; it had no known smell, just a cold, chalky smell. The puppy didn't want it, didn't need it, didn't know it. Suddenly his nose was thrust into the cold milk. 'Got to show them how at first,' the man's voice said.

Cold sticky milk stuffed his nostrils. The puppy

choked, spluttered milk. 'Now look, John, what you made him do!' the woman screeched. 'Two minutes in the house and already two messes on my clean floor, and I've just waxed it.'

Now the boy grabbed the puppy. The boy rubbed his hand over the puppy's nose, rubbing away the cold stickiness of the milk. The puppy sneezed.

'You can't coddle him too much. Start out that way and you'll soon have a dog nobody can do anything with,' the father instructed. 'Try him with some warm milk, he's not used to cold milk.'

There was the saucer again, the milk, white and thin with a little steaminess curling up from it. But now the puppy was afraid of the white saucer. He squirmed under the hand that shoved him towards the milk. He whined when he couldn't squirm free; he bared his sharp little teeth.

'See that? See that? Wanted to bite me. He's got spirit all right,' the man exclaimed. The big sure voice knew all about puppies, and what should be done. 'Well, we'll have to cure him of that. Break their spirit first, then build it up again – your way. That's the way to get a good trained dog. Of course, you can't start yet, he's too young . . . So we'll just teach him to drink first.' The puppy's face was shoved into the milk, the hand pressed down. The puppy choked, he struggled, his nails scrabbled on the smooth linoleum. Milk got in his eyes.

'Maybe he isn't hungry,' the little girl said in a tiny, wretched voice. 'Please, Dad . . .'

'Puppies are always hungry,' the man's sure voice said. 'He's just not weaned yet. You two take him back for a week or so. Then when you get him again he won't be so helpless and we can start training him a bit.'

The girl and boy began to cry.

Of course, the puppy understood none of this. He knew nothing of laughter and weeping and talk. It only added to his bewilderment and coldness. That is what he understood the best – the coldness which meant being separated from his mother. He was sprawling on the cold floor, forgotten by the weeping children who were pleading with their father. The father softened. 'All right, all right! You two win, we'll keep him, feed him with a medicine dropper if we have to – just so you stop your blubbering. But one thing – see to it that you help your mother take care of him.'

'Ha, it's easy for you to talk,' the woman said. 'I'm the one that's going to have the mess. They'll fuss the little animal half to death the first couple of days, but once the novelty is worn off . . .'

The children broke off their sobbing; they'd won. Everybody at the same time remembered the puppy.

'Now where'd he crawl to?'

He had crawled to a dark space between the stove and the wall. There was a little warmth there. The little dog sat pressed against the stove, hugging the slight feeling of warmth that seeped through the oven wall from the oven pilot light. They found him.

'Now why'd he crawl there? Look quick, I suppose he went there to make a mess again,' the woman said.

A big hand reached into the narrow space. The puppy pressed back against the wall. But the hand came on. The puppy growled, bared his teeth, desperately scared of the poking hand. He growled little puppy growls, warning the hand away.

'Listen to that, will you?' the woman said, half-amused, half in alarm. 'He wanted to bite me! He isn't going to be a mean dog, is he?'

Later quiet came, and the dark, and the cold – except

for the feeble seeping warmth from the oven of the gas stove. The puppy was in the narrow space, the first place where he had felt a little warmth and a little safety. But now the house was quiet and strange and hostile. There were no voices now, only deep breathings from behind a closed door. The puppy scrabbled at the old sweater the little girl had shoved into the space between the wall and the stove. He rumpled it; he tried to snuggle into it; he crawled under a sleeve but his little head emerged from the other side of the sleeve. Then the loose sweater slipped away from him entirely over the waxy floor, it was gone. The puppy raised his head and whined out his misery and loneliness. When he had started he could not stop the whine; it shrieked higher and higher, and in it were all his loneliness, coldness and fear.

There were stumbling noises. The man's hard voice clapped into the little space beside the stove. 'Quiet. Quiet, you . . .'

It flattened the puppy, scared the whining out of him until there was only the thin tickle of a whimper left down in his throat. 'I know you're homesick, but I've got to sleep, I've got to go to work in the morning.' The reasonableness left the voice in the irritation of disrupted sleep. 'You're going to make a din wherever you are, so down into the cellar you go. I've got to get some sleep.'

The man jerked the puppy out of the corner. Barefooted and sleepy the man went down cellar steps, pulled a cardboard box from somewhere, fumbled around, found some newspapers and rags, dropped them to the bottom of the box, dropped the puppy on top of them. The light went out, the cellar door was shoved shut, darkness settled in the cellar, darkness in the box. The first whimper came squeezing out of the puppy's throat. It rose. It bounced back at him from the four sides of the box and echoed away in the deep cellar. The echo fooled him, made him stop to listen. It was almost as if he'd heard a brother puppy whimper back. And then it rose up out of him, higher, higher, without let-up, tearing his little throat. He couldn't stop it. Only his mother, his home, his nest could stop it.

Soft careful noises came down the cellar steps. Bare feet were carefully feeling their way down the dark steps. There were cautious whispers. There were the little girl and boy, fearful in the dark gloom of the cellar, fearful of being heard by the parents. And then the puppy was cuddled in a warm lap; warm, soft hands stroked him. There they sat, shivering, whispering, loving.

The cellar door ripped open. Light flooded the basement. 'John, they're here. Down in the cellar with that dog!'

The man came, sleepy, yawning. 'How long have you two been down there?'

'Oh, we just came, Daddy . . .'

'What a night, what a night,' the man was grumbling. 'Well, back to bed with you, and don't you ever dare to do that again.'

'But, Dad, he cried so.'

'Well, you can't sit up with him nights. Back to your beds right now.'

'But he'll cry so.' The boy, George, was almost crying himself.

'All right,' his mother said at last. 'I'll put a hot-water bottle in with him, and wrap it in that old piece of fur of mine. If I do that, will you promise to go right back to sleep?'

'Oh, yes, Mama.'

They all disappeared. Later the woman came back alone and started fussing in the deep cardboard box. She was yawning and shivering. 'You must be dead tired yourself, you little silly. Go to sleep now.'

Soothed into it by the warmth rising up from the hot-water bottle under the piece of fur; fooled by the fur – dead fur, but live, lovely warmth – he slept.

4. THE BROOM

That was the first day of Candy's new life. Candy, the children had called him, because they loved him so, and what is nicer than candy? Besides, his brown and white coat did look like candy. The softness of his puppy fur made the sandy brown splotches among the white look like butterscotch, if you had a child's imagination, and if you loved him so.

The two children were Candy's whole life. There was the brief half-hour in the morning, hectic with breakfast and getting up and getting ready for school.

That little half-hour the children were with him in the kitchen, and he was with them and around their feet. Busy and confused as things were then, there still was stolen time for some nice words, quick little whispered promises, quick pettings, and even quicker, hurried kisses. Even the boy kissed Candy when his sister wasn't around. They both kissed him when their mother wasn't looking – a quick moist kiss right on his moist cold nose, and then they were gone to school.

Then began the day without the children. It would drag lonesomely and tediously into the afternoon. Late in the afternoon the children returned, and everything became wonderful with life and love and happiness again. But the after-school hours were so happy and busy with romping, running, dashing, growling games, that they too were gone in a wink.

In between the two brief periods of happiness stretched the school day. Of course, the puppy knew nothing of school; to him it was the long day, with the children gone. The long day with the house silent and empty of talk and laughter and petting and little tussles. The long day with only the woman in the house – the woman and the broom.

The warm, furry mother, the puppy brothers and sisters, the nest in the blanket, had long since slipped out of the puppy's milky memory. This was his new home, the children were his new happiness, but his comfort was the small warm space between the stove and wall. It was his comfort, his fort, and his haven of refuge. Outside the little corner in all the rest of the house were the woman and the broom.

In the dark narrow space beside the stove he felt bravest. It was his hide-out to slink and crawl into when he had done wrong. And often he did wrong, he did many things wrong, for he still did not understand many things. He didn't understand, and then he did wrong, and then he was punished. Then there was only the little warm space beside the stove for his comfort.

Outside the little corner, in all the enormous house, ranged the woman. She was all about the house, everywhere he heard her, high up and far away, and then again criss-crossing back and forth through the kitchen, where he sat in his little corner. She never stooped to him, her voice did not caress his ears, her hand did not stroke him. Oh, sometimes when working in the kitchen she petted him, but hastily, her mind not on it, always with other things on her mind. Always there were things hurrying her, the meals, the washing, the cleaning of the house. Now and then she petted him when he had done right. He did not understand, did not know when he had done right – it just happened. He did not know when he had done wrong – that just happened, too. But when he had done wrong there came the terror of the broom to teach him right from wrong.

The terrible broom came, swept him over the waxy floor. The broom came to find him, poke him, punish him. He would crawl out before it, flattened, frightened, cringing. And when the broom prodded, it stabbed and hurt, and while the broom hurt the woman's sharp, screeching voice lashed him. He would crawl out before her and the broom, weak with fear, no strength at all in his legs, swimming on his rubbery legs over the polished linoleum towards his gas-stove corner. Always towards his corner, for it was his fort and his refuge and his comfort. And there he felt a little bit brave.

It never did any good. The evil broom could find him even in his corner. The broom came, poked him, prodded him. Didn't she know that the stiff, sharp straws of the broom pierced his thin puppy hide? Didn't she know? It hurt, oh, viciously – all the raw needle stabs of the broom.

There was no getting away from it. The broom sought him out and worsted him. But the corner was still his fort, and when the broom attacked and had him against the wall, then at last he fought back in his terror – snarling puppy snarls, bared puppy fangs, bit into the broom.

Always he lost to the broom, but in his terror he fought and snarled and bit. Didn't she know that? Didn't she know he had to fight back in his terror?

She didn't know, because she was a little afraid herself. When he fought and growled and bit, her voice became loud and hard and ugly because she was afraid of the puppy.

'There's a mean streak in you,' she'd yell. 'A couple months old and snarling and biting. When you grow bigger the children won't be safe with you. But I'll get it out of you. There! There!' The broom came again and again. 'There. Now will you behave?'

Until at last he subsided in a stupor of terror before the prodding broom. A terror too big for growling and biting, that left nothing but an abject begging and pleading that could be uttered only in a shrieking puppy whine. 'There,' she'd say at last, and then and then only would she put the broom away. By then he had often messed up his corner, and then, if she noticed, the broom came back, and then came still more terror. Didn't she know he did it in fear and terror? Didn't she know he didn't want to foul his beloved corner? It was his home, his fort, his haven of refuge, and his only little possession. Didn't she know?

At last the punishment was over. The woman would set the broom in its corner; she'd hurry away to her work. But the broom's corner was opposite the little dog's corner. There stood the hideous broom. He could see it from where he still lay, squashed back against the wall. Long after the broom stood still, he lay there pleading with the broom, lifting his meek brown eyes to the lifeless broom.

Sometimes he did not dare come out of his corner because of the broom in the other corner. But sometimes the seeping warmth of the gas stove wasn't comfort enough. Then he had to dare to go out in spite of the broom, slink out and sneak away in search of something of the children's. It might be anything – a cap, a muffler, a little sweater – just something that belonged to them and was a little like them because it smelled of them. And if he found it he dragged it back to his corner for comfort. He would snuggle in it for warmth and love, because his little quaking flanks were still cold with fear.

But he just had a little puppy mind, and after the quakings and terror had drained out of him, he would start to play with the cap or muffler or sweater, because this was the children's. When his fear had all seeped away, he'd shake the sweater or muffler, tussle with it, fight it with sharp little teeth, gnaw it. Didn't he have to be brave again in his corner after all his terror?

The woman would come quietly into the kitchen, hearing his puppy growls as, full of big, heroic puppy imagination, he mauled the sweater or muffler to its death. He would be so busy, and then he would look up, and there would be her face poking into the narrow opening. All the little growls would die in him, and the fear would crawl into his tail, and his tail would crawl between his legs, and he would squash himself against the wall. For dragging things from other parts of the house she had a different punishment for him. After she'd pulled the muffler or sweater or cap away from him, she'd put the terrifying broom across the opening of his narrow space, and lock him in. There he would sit, pressed against the wall, eyes fixed and staring on the terrible broom, until limp and exhausted from fear, he would slide down the wall and sink into a little puppy heap in puppy sleep. A troubled, broom-haunted sleep in which his paws twitched nervously because in his sleep he was fleeing from the fearful broom.

But always it would come again – the brief period of his happiness. The children would return from school to romp and play with him. They'd take him out into the yard, and the yard would be full of their noise, their voices and his barking. They calling: 'Candy, Candy, Candy.' He running and tearing and tumbling in his eagerness to do everything and be everywhere at once for them. 'Candy, Candy, Candy.' And the whole yard full of happiness and play and love.

All in a moment the brief after-school hours of play would end. The man would come home, and everything would change again. The children had to go in the house, and they'd eat in another room, and he would be relegated to the kitchen.

The little dog stood in a humble fear of the big man, different from his cringing fear of the woman and his abject terror of the broom. The man was only there in the evening, and since the children were there in the evening, too, it made the man less fearsome. The woman was there in the evening, too, the woman was always there, but it was different. In the evening the big hard man with the big hard voice was in control.

Somehow the puppy sensed that the man meant well, but the man had hard hands, a hard voice, hard-handed ways. He handled the little dog hard, squeezed him too hard, stroked him too hard, so that the soft little pliable puppy body almost caved in under the stroking. The man petted too hard, and when he was through with his petting, he dropped him too hard.

And then there was his big thunderous voice. 'Into the kitchen! Into the kitchen! Into your corner!'

When that thunderous order came, whatever the puppy was doing, whatever he was playing with the children, he'd have to stop it at that moment, and go crawling alone to the kitchen and his corner. Even if the children still held him, he squirmed away to obey, he sensed that before the man and his thundering orders the children were as helpless as he. He could not even hesitate on his way to the kitchen, linger or look back over his shoulder in his yearning for one of the children to call him back. 'What did I say? Get into that kitchen! Into your corner!'

He had to go, the faster the better.

'That's the way to train a young dog,' the father would lecture the children. 'He's got to know who is boss. You don't have to slap him or beat him, just that command in your voice. You kids coddle him too much. Do you want a sissy dog? I like a dog to be all dog.'

'Yes, Father,' the children would say. 'Dad, may we go in the kitchen now and play?' What they meant, of course, was play with their Candy.

Sometimes they might. The children would come. In one quiver of delight he would come pelting out of his corner. In a moment all three would be in a tussle all over the kitchen floor. But soon all three would forget in their fun, soon they would be romping all through the house. Always in the midst of it, like a thunder crash out of nowhere, would come the voice: 'What did I say? What did I tell you? Into the kitchen! Into your corner!'

Often the little dog's crashing fright amidst the noisy fun would be so huge, so sudden, he would mess up the floor. In his shame and terror he would swim belly-flat to the kitchen and his corner. Then the woman's words would begin to fly, the words lashing him as he crawled in shame. The two helpless children would desperately try to cover up for him.

'Oh, Mother, please. It was our fault, we forgot and took him out of the kitchen. Please, Mother, we're cleaning it up ...'

After such an accident there was no pardon for him, no reprieve. He stayed in his corner. The evening had to ooze away in the corner, his ears constantly prick-ing for the slightest sound from the children in the innocent puppy hope that they would come and play with him. They did not come, and he sat yearning in the corner. And in the other corner of the silent kitchen stood the broom.

That was his puppy life. He lived from day to day in humble fear of the man, in cringing fear of the woman, and in terror of the broom. There were only two good things in his little life – the two children. The children were lovely. He lived for them. He might forget and do wrong again and again, he might not understand and do wrong a thousand times, but that one thing he understood – their love for him, his love for them. It all but consumed his little heart.

5. THE RIDE

An early spring day came which brought an enormous event into the puppy's young life – his first ride in a car. The too early spring day lured the family into going for a ride into the country. The day was full of spring balminess, full of the large promise of warm days to come, budding and blooming and sunny friendliness.

He was to go, too. Candy had to go, the children had wheedled and insisted. If they were going into the country and stopping at Grandpa's and Grandma's, they would simply have to take Candy. Why, if it hadn't been for Grandpa and Grandma they could never have bought their little puppy!

There was no denying them. The parents yielded. The girl carried Candy to the car, she hugged him against her in her delight and triumph. They were to have Candy with them in the back seat.

The woman got into the front seat. The father slid in behind the wheel. Immediately there started an enormous roar. It flattened the puppy in the girl's lap. But the motor roar softened into purring motion, the car slid down the street. It was an enormous experience – that soft, effortless, swift motion of the car. Candy quivered. He wasn't running, his short legs weren't pumping, but still he was rushing down the street. It was unbelievable and wonderful. He couldn't lie flat now. He jumped up in the girl's lap and poked his cold nose against the window to see, to know this speed. It couldn't be believed.

'Catherine, open that window. Look how he's smearing it! And I had them so clean.' It was the woman's fretting, irritated voice. Something clean was getting dirty. This time he paid it no attention, he was too excited.

The little girl obediently opened the window. Now there was the sound of the wind rushing. He had to have his head out of that window, but the little girl held him back, afraid that in his excitement he might push right out of the car. He wriggled and squirmed. Now, now his head was out of the window and in the slip stream of the wind rushing along the car. He was sure he was running, fast, oh, fast as a big dog! He could imagine it, the wind in his ears. He panted with the excitement.

They laughed at him. It was a nice laugh in the closeness of the car. A nice soft laugh, and he heard it in the slip stream of the wind. It added to his excitement. He pulled his head in, looked at them all, pleased and confused. He felt pleased with himself, he felt bold, like a big dog. But he had to poke his head out of the window again.

'Oh, Mother, you ought to feel his heart go.'

'Let me feel,' the boy demanded.

'He thinks he's quite a big shot now, don't you, Candy?' The man was talking to him. With his ears outside in the rush of the wind he could hear it. He pulled his head in to look bewilderedly at the man. Immediately he had to get his head out again, the wind in his ears, his nose into the thousand odours streaming by, all new, all exciting. The girl held him too tightly. He couldn't breathe that way, and he had to pant in all this rushing. He got out of her grip, jumped to the boy's side of the car, jumped up against the window. He had to see everything, know everything. Hurry up, open that window.

The boy laughed and opened the window. The boy didn't hold him back! The puppy stood up on his trampling excited hind legs on the boy's lap and reached way out.

They all watched him, chuckling at his antics. 'I believe he's finally growing up and getting some sense,' the woman said. 'Maybe the worst is over. He's getting house-trained.'

The car stopped for a light. There was a dog waiting on the curb, huge, muscled, a giant. But looking down in his excitement from the high safety of the car, in the safe bold feeling of all his people around him, the puppy suddenly found himself barking at the big dog. He rattled his little high-pitched barks. The light changed, the car started up. With the car moving away he peered back, sent a last threatening growl after the huge dog. The car roared with laughter.

He pulled his head in, sat on the boy's lap, looking in bewilderment from the one to the other. Bewildered, but feeling proud of himself, big and competent. Somehow he sensed he had done something very right, not wrong.

'Well, I'll be blowed,' the man was spluttering. 'You little idiot! But that's the spirit. We'll make a dog out of you yet. Took no nonsense from that big dog, did you? Left him with a reminder you'd be back to take care of him some day.'

He sat with his head cocked, listening. He had done something enormously right, more right than ever before. It was a big, proud feeling. But the car was gaining speed. He had to get his head out of the window. He did not trample in excitement now. He stood rigid, legs tensed, waiting for another dog to growl at, for he had somehow done something very right.

The boy tickled him. He pulled his head in for a moment, gave the boy's face a hasty lick. The boy pummelled him. He sank his teeth in the sleeve of the boy's sweater. He loved them all. It was such a good feeling that he had to bite and gnaw and shake the woolly arm.

When he returned to the window, they were in the country. Long flat fields were rushing along, and in them stood enormous animals ten times bigger than the big dog. He quivered and stared in awe, too awed to bark. It was the most tremendous experience in his little life.

He pulled his head in and sat very still, trying to absorb it in his puppy brain. He was staring straight ahead at the back of the woman's neck. All of a sudden his little tail waggled; he balanced on the boy's knee, reached way out, and gave the woman's neck a timid lick.

She felt it. She turned around and smiled at him. 'Ah, you're all right,' she said. 'You're going to be all right.'

He knew it, and he was grateful in his eager little heart. She was going to be all right, too. Everything was going to be all right. He loved them all.

They rode along. 'Oh, will you look at this weather,' the woman suddenly burst out. 'Why, it's still winter according to the calendar. A lot the calendar knows! But isn't it unbelievable?' She looked all around, she breathed it in. 'It's so good.'

Her husband looked over the fields. 'Too good, if you ask me. That sky isn't healthy out there in the south-west. Always watch that south-west corner — that's the rain and storm corner.'

The woman turned around to the children. 'Listen to the farmer talking now that we're going back to his old farm. We don't get there five times a year, but just as soon as we're on the way he knows all about the weather and everything again.'

The puppy wriggled. He loved her new relaxed voice. The same gratefulness seemed to be in her voice that was in his little heart. The woman noticed his squirmings. 'Look,' she said, 'are you making eyes at me? Trying to smooch me! You're an old smoocher.' The puppy danced and wriggled, his little heart thumped, he wanted to lick her all over, he couldn't reach her. But she reached back and patted his head. The day was good.

The car slowed at last. Now it made a turn up a gravel drive to a house that stood well back from the road. An old brown and white hound, sunning himself on a sack against the wall of a shed, reluctantly rose to his feet, came stiffly across the yard to the car. Before the big dog got there, two old people came hurrying out of the house and were beside the car, reaching in to shake hands, talking excitedly to the big people in front, calling to the children in back. 'Oh, Grandpa . . . Hello, Grandma,' the children babbled back fondly. The boy eagerly held up the puppy, but in the excitement of the greetings the old folks did not see the little dog. The boy and girl sat on the edge of the seat, waiting to spring their surprise.

'That's what I like about spring,' the old man was saying outside the car. 'It brings back the birds and it brings out the city people.'

'Oh, go on with you, Dad,' the children's mother said. 'We were here three times last winter, and in some pretty bad weather, too. To be honest, we hadn't really intended to come today, but the children were bound and determined, they just had to show off their new puppy.'

The boy and girl looked at each other. Their mother had spoiled the surprise.

'Well, so you finally got around to getting them a puppy,' the old man was saying.

'We!' the father said. 'It was you put them up to it. And their grandma, stuffing money into every note she wrote. I can tell you it all went into the piggy bank – not a cent for candy. Guess that's why they called the pup Candy – they'd gone without so long.'

'Candy!' the old man exclaimed. 'What a right name. Only a child would think of such a name. Now all the name I could ever think of for any dog I ever had was Butch.' He tried to peer round the woman's shoulder to see the little dog. He beamed at the children. 'I'm glad,' he told them.

'A dog is good for kids,' he told the children's parents.

'Maybe,' his daughter-in-law said. 'But a puppy isn't good for the house, or the tempers.'

'You and that clean house of yours,' the old man said impatiently. 'But come on, come into our house. I don't know how clean it is, but I've got to see that Candy they're keeping hid in that back seat.'

'But, Grandpa, won't old Butch . . .?' the girl quavered doubtfully. Nobody heard her. The old hound stood between the old woman and the old man, silent, gravely watchful, just half-accepting the new people. The girl got out of the car ahead of her brother to shield Candy from old Butch's sight. But the old man snatched the puppy out of the boy's arms. He held him high. He crowed up at him. 'So you are Candy? So the children belong to you? Well, what a nice little dog. Look at him, Grandma!'

'Ah,' the old woman said. 'Oh, I'm glad,' she told the children.

All the attention for the puppy was suddenly too much for the old hound. He made a silly whining jealous noise in his throat. Then, half-ashamed, he changed it to a stiff growl. He stood rigid, threatening growls pushing up out of his throat, his eyes mean.

The sudden growling beneath him unnerved the puppy. His tail pasted between his hanging legs, he whimpered. The puppy's whining enraged the old dog; he reared up.

'Butch, down. Butch, behave,' the old lady ordered.

The old dog stood down, stood silent.

The puppy went on whimpering. He tried to crawl away into the old man. Suddenly, even with his face hidden under the old man's arm, he yelped out in terror. The old man put a comforting hand over the puppy's trembling back, but the little dog whined on.

'What have you been doing to this little fellow?' the old man demanded. He looked at the woman. 'It's all right for a puppy to get scared at the first sight of a big strange dog, but he stays scared. He doesn't even feel safe with me, and Butch hasn't moved. Why, he's all mouse inside. It's no good.'

He got no answer, and he hastily remembered his manners. 'Well, come into the house – Candy and all. We're just keeping you standing here.'

'He isn't quite house trained yet,' the woman warned her father-in-law.

'What of it,' the old man said. 'Houses are for people and dogs.'

'Listen to him,' the old lady said. 'He's never had to keep a house clean. My, but I'm glad you came, such a perfect day.'

'It isn't going to stay so perfect,' the old man announced. 'Have you been noticing that bank in the south-west?'

Nobody paid any attention; they trooped into the house behind each other, chattering. The children hung back at the kitchen doorway, waiting to see what Butch would do. The old dog turned away, slowly went back to his sack against the shed.

'Grandpa likes Candy, doesn't he?' the girl said proudly.

The puppy had gone to sleep in the old man's lap. The children hovered beside his chair, disappointed that their pride in the puppy was so neglected in all the grown-up talk. The children stayed close, but they did not quite dare to take the puppy out of their grandfather's lap.

Their grandmother at last noticed it in the midst of her talk with her daughter-in-law. 'He's sweet, that puppy of yours,' she told the children. 'You can bring him here when old Butch gives out. Butch is reaching his end, but then he's eighteen now.'

'Eighteen, what do you mean?' the old man corrected. 'Nineteen.'

'Going on nineteen,' she said firmly.

'Is Butch that old?' the girl exclaimed. She was struck by it. 'Why, if we have Candy that long, I'll be a woman like Mother.'

'I'll be a man,' George said loudly, not wanting to be outdone by his sister.

Their mother looked up from studying some new curtains she had in her lap. 'Please don't talk that way. It sounds almost scary.'

'They grow up though, and go away,' the old lady said softly. She looked at her son, immersed in crop talk with his father. She turned her attention back to the curtains under discussion. 'I thought these would go well with our high narrow windows,' she said. The two women talked eagerly.

The boy and girl hung around behind the chairs. The puppy went on sleeping. The time dragged in the house of the old people among the old grown-up talk. There was little to do but munch their grandmother's cookies. 'We're going out,' the boy announced. 'We're going to show Candy the barn, and even the fields.'

Only his mother noticed. 'No, you stay right here. You've no boots, and the ground's thawed and messy. You stay here.'

Disconsolately they wandered to the window. Beyond the narrow window the fields stretched warm and sweet in the spring sunlight. In the yard old Butch got up, pawed heavily at his sack to rumple it, and plopped down again.

'He's twice as old as you are,' the girl told her brother.

'Pretty near twice as old as you are, too,' the boy said resentfully.

'Yes, but I'm a year and three months older than you.'

They made talk that they weren't interested in. They were really listening for changes in the adult conversation that would indicate the visit was about to break up. At last their father scraped his chair back. 'Well,' he announced, 'if we're going to enjoy some of that sunshine . . .' He yawned and stretched. The children came eagerly from the window. The boy was bold enough now to take the sleeping puppy from his grandfather's lap. 'Itching to go, aren't you?' the old man laughed. 'Old people aren't much fun, are they?'

'Oh, no, Grandpa,' the boy said dutifully, 'but we'd figured we could take Candy all over the farm, but it's too muddy.' He looked at his mother.

'Sure, I know,' the grandfather said. 'Sure, it's nearly always too muddy for a boy and a dog.'

'Yes,' the boy said.

'Are we going back the same way?' Catherine asked. 'I hope not,' she told her brother when no one took notice of her question.

They followed the grown-ups to the car and were relieved when old Butch did not bother to raise more

43

than his head from the sack. They hurried into the car, sat impatient with the elaborate leave-taking of the adults. The sleepy puppy curled himself in the boy's lap and dozed again. Now at last the car started. At last they were going down the drive.

Then the car stopped again. Grandfather was shouting something, hands cupped to his mouth. He pointed to the south-west sky and they guessed that he was warning them about the storm threat. They all nodded. They all looked towards the south-west sky. The sunlight was still warm over all the country, but there seemed to be a strange glassiness to it. 'Whatever's sitting there, it isn't healthy, and it's coming. But we'll be home long before it breaks,' the father said.

The car started up once more. 'Come back soon with Candy,' the grandmother shrilled. They could hear her piercing voice plainly.

'We will. Oh, we will, Grandma,' the children chorused. 'Bye, Grandpa.' They waved their hands very hard.

The puppy awoke, and looked back at the two old people. He wagged his tail.

6. THE BRIDGE

They were on the road again, on the way home now, the farm of the two old people was long out of sight. The girl leaned forward. 'Dad,' she urged, 'let's go a long way around on our way home.'

'I don't know,' her mother said doubtfully. 'Your dad and grandfather seem to think there's going to be rain. I left the bedroom windows open.'

'Oh, it won't come that soon,' the man said knowingly. 'I'll just take them around some of these little roads I used to roam as a kid. Show them some real back country.'

'Oh, good!'

There were many roads, and many turns. The car turned at last from a gravel road into a narrower dirt road. The little road wound in a confusion of turns into deep wooded country, the road became little more than a track. There were wooded stretches where the roots of trees protruded from the steep, washed-out banks. The fenders of the car almost scraped them as the car bumped along.

'I hope you know where you're going,' the woman said. 'And where we are, for that matter. I don't know any more which is east and which is west.'

The filtered light in the car was shadowy and sombre as the deep road descended a heavily wooded hill dark with pine trees. But it wasn't the pine trees alone that made the road shadowy and dark. The sun briefly reappeared. Then a sombre shadowiness fell into the place of the too brief, too glassy green glare of the momentary sunlight. The road and wooded hill suddenly looked threatening.

'We'd better find a good highway as soon as possible, and start for home,' the woman said doubtfully.

'Oh, no, this is exciting. It's wild,' the girl said.

'It's the Wild West,' the boy said. 'We're cowboys.'

His father laughed. 'Cowboys? Well, it feels like cowboys, the way we're bouncing around. What a road! Don't they ever scrape it?'

'We haven't got a flat tyre, have we?' the mother said sharply.

'No, it's the road,' the man said. He was feeling his way, easing the car down the long steep descent. They bounced into a pot-hole and out again. The puppy bumped his nose sharply against the edge of the

45

window. He whimpered. The girl took him in her arms.

'John, it *is* a flat tyre!' the woman said.

Now at last they were at the bottom of the long hill. The car was crossing an old wooden bridge over a creek. Under the wheels the bridge boards slapped up, jarred thunderously back into place.

'It's only the boards,' the man muttered aloud to himself, but now there was doubt in his voice. 'Maybe I'd better have a look.' He stopped the car just across the bridge, and got out.

He came back to the window. 'It *is* a flat.'

'I knew it. I told you so,' the woman said stiffly.

'So you knew it. It's still a flat, and I'd still have had to come down here. You can't jack up a car on a hill like that.'

They all got out of the car and stood staring at the flat, dispirited tyre that had come part way off its rim.

'At least the sun *is* shining again,' the woman said in a moody attempt to be cheerful.

The man was ripping things out of the trunk. 'Rain is all we'd need. Isn't it supposed to rain when you've a flat?' He tried to make a joke of it, but his voice was vicious.

'Can I help, Dad?'

'Yes, George, grab the pump and see if the spare tyre will come up.'

'Is that flat, too?' the woman demanded. 'John, you'd think you'd check on things like that. Taking us into wild country like this without even a good spare!'

The man's head was thrust deep into the trunk; he was scrabbling in its far reaches for tools. He flung them out behind him as he found them. The jack came flying, struck the road, bounced up and hit the girl in the shins. 'Dad!' she shrieked. She half-started to cry. She tried to stoop and rub her leg with the puppy clutched in her arm.

'Well, stay out of the way then,' the man barked. 'Get back in the car, you and your mother. I don't know anything more useless than women with a flat tyre.' He looked at his wife. She walked silently back to the car.

The girl started to follow her mother. On sudden impulse she turned and carried the puppy to the bridge. From the bridge girl and dog looked down into a sand-bottomed creek that had cut deep into its wooded banks. The puppy began trembling with excitement at the sight of water rushing and swirling below him. Sunlight sparkled in the creek. Through the sunny water a black object came rushing and twirling. It disappeared under the bridge. The puppy struggled to get free from the girl's arms. 'Shall we go down to the creek?' the girl asked him.

With the puppy in her arms she left the bridge and went carefully down a deep gully at the side of the road. The dry gully that had been cut by rainwater sweeping down the hill was difficult and steep and rutted. Clutching the puppy against her, the girl worked her way down. It was exciting.

Near the bottom of the gully, even in this desolate place, was a heap of rubbish. An old dishevelled broom lay sprawled across the rubbish pile. The girl had to lift her feet high to get over the jagged rubbish heap. She tripped over the broom. To keep on her feet she had to make the last part of the descent in a breathless, unwilling run that stopped her at the very edge of the water. 'There, we made it,' she gasped. 'There's your creek you wanted to go to . . . We almost went in it.' She set the quivering puppy down. 'There's your creek.'

The puppy dashed to the creek. A swirling piece of

bark came racing by on the water. It was running away from him! He barked at it excitedly. Now it dodged under the dark bridge to get away from him. He gave chase. The girl ran after him. 'Careful, Candy, don't get in the creek. It would sweep you away, and I'd never find you again.'

It was dark and mysterious under the wooden bridge. The creek roared hollowly under the planking. Up above, but sounding far away among the rushing sounds of the water, the girl could hear the noises of the tyre being changed. There was the clank of tools. It was mysterious here, dark and brooding. It was as if she'd suddenly disappeared from the earth, but there was the sunlight in the creek to reassure her. The puppy quivered against her leg, excited to the tip of his tail by the rush and roar of water. A tuft of dried grass came flinging by; he rushed at it in mad little rushes, barking brave, furious puppy barks. 'Isn't this fun?' the girl said excitedly. 'Nobody knows we're here. They can't see us or hear us.'

With her toe she pushed an old rusted coffee can into the creek, watched the water grab it and swirl it out from the darkness under the bridge into the sunlit creek beyond. It spun, hit a tree root, bubbled and sank. The girl stood watching the spot as if half-expecting the coffee can to come bobbing up again. As she stared the sunlit creek beyond the bridge turned dark.

Almost the next moment a sweep of hail boiled into the water. Hail bulleted down on the planks of the bridge above her, the hail changed to rain and became one single harsh sweeping noise on the planking. The first big muddy drops began dripping through the cracks between the boards.

'It's raining! We've got to get out of here. It's going to storm.' A clap of unexpected thunder crashed down on the bridge. It echoed enormously in the dark hollow place. The girl staggered back as if she had been hit. She stood petrified, hands pressed over her eyes, as lightning flashed. 'Daddy, Mother,' she whimpered. Lightning flashed again. 'Dad!' She started running from under the bridge, tore up the steep

gully. But the gully had become slippery with rain. She tripped, fell flat. She screamed but blindly scrambled up again. The old broom slid down beside her. Whimpering with fear, she struggled up the gully. The rain water gushed down. The whole front of her coat, her hands were wet and slimy.

Above her on the road she heard tools being flung into the car, heard car doors slam shut. She scrambled wildly towards the sound. 'Mother, Daddy, oh, don't leave me.'

'Catherine!' her mother was shrieking out of the car. 'Catherine, where are you?'

'Candy, come on,' the girl babbled hysterically. 'Candy, come on!' She scrabbled up the wet, slippery gully almost on hands and knees, desperately looking up into the driving rain for a first sight of the car.

'Catherine!'

'I'm coming. I'm coming. Candy, come on.'

'Well, come on!' Her father was also shouting now. Now that they had heard her, knew where she was, their voices became angry, impatient.

'CATHERINE!'

A clap of thunder filled the wooded hill, a sizzle of lightning fell down behind it, leaped whitely above the gloomy tree tops. Then thunder rolled again. The tree tops swept back and forth in a sudden gale of wind. The whimpering girl clawed her way to the top of the gully. Now she could see the car. She pulled herself on to the road, dashed to the car and flung herself in.

'Look at you, look at you,' her mother cried out.

The girl looked down at herself. She started to cry. Her father turned. 'Now what was the idea of going off with a storm threatening?'

'Where is Candy? What did you do with Candy?' the boy demanded. Lightning flashed again.

The girl stared about her. 'Candy?' she asked bewilderedly. 'Didn't he follow me? He was right behind me . . . Oh, I left him there,' she wailed as the sudden knowledge flooded her that in her hysteria she had never looked back for the little dog after she had fallen. 'I fell and slipped and I got scared, and it rained so and the lightning, and I couldn't make it up that slippery gully . . .'

'If you couldn't make it, how did you expect Candy to?' the boy started to shout. He stopped, he had the door open, he was halfway out when his father grabbed him. 'You stay here. You can't go down there. Look at that water washing down that hill.'

The girl opened the window. 'Candy, Candy, Candy,' she shrieked out into the rain.

The wind swept rain into her face and open mouth, swept it through the car.

'Close that window!'

The girl closed it. 'Oh, oh, oh,' she moaned. She rocked herself in her woe. Suddenly she was still. 'Mother,' she announced, 'it's my fault, and I'm all wet and muddy anyway, and he'll drown there.'

She was out of the car in that moment, scared and desperate enough to defy both her mother and father. They yelled her name, yelled fierce orders for her to come back. She did not listen, but ran to the gully. At the edge of the road she stopped helplessly; the rain water was gushing down the gully in a muddy torrent. 'Candy, Candy,' she screamed down the bank.

She stood hunched up, bowed against the rain and wind, listening. It seemed to her that among the rush of water she heard an answering whine from under the bridge. Then lightning sizzled close, thunder rolled. She listened again after the thunder peal. But a savage bolt of lightning falling almost directly into the preceding thunder frightened her. In terror she started to rush back to the car. Instead she dashed towards the other side of the road, plunged down the embankment there, slipped, but clung to a bush halfway down the bank. She held herself up by the bush, shrieking: 'Candy, Candy, Candy.'

Ahead of the car a large jagged chunk of half-thawed dirt and gravel broke away from the side of the road and plopped down the embankment. The rain water immediately filled the hole, made a little cataract as it plunged down the bank to the creek.

'John, look at that!' the woman shrieked. 'The road's breaking up.'

The man started the car, hastily drove it to the middle of the road. The girl down the embankment heard the car start. 'Dad, Dad,' she screamed.

She threw herself up the bank, came running hysterically. The car stopped. The girl threw herself in. 'I . . . I thought you were going to leave me behind.'

'No, the road's washing away. We've got to get out of here.'

The boy started silently crying, eyes tightly shut, fists clenched.

The storm and the wind swooped down again. Rain changed to hail once more. They could hear the water in its downhill rush washing against the wheels of the car. All of a sudden the road and wooded hill were one mass of blinding lightning.

The woman cowered in the front seat. 'John, John, if you don't take me out of here, I'll go mad. I can't stand it.' A square of thawed gravel and dirt broke off from the side of the road again. 'Look!' the woman screamed. 'And all for one miserable dog. Why didn't he come then? Can't you come back when the storm is over? Do you want Catherine to catch her death of pneumonia sitting there soaked to the skin? Why don't you take me home?' A new crash of lightning scared her into silence. She began to cry softly.

The man looked desperate. He flung his door open. 'Candy, Candy,' he bellowed into the storm. The woman began screaming along with him. 'Candy, Candy, Candy.' But outside the car there was only the sound of the rushing water. 'I'm going down there,' the man said. 'I'll get him.'

'You are not!' the woman shrieked. 'Suppose something happened to you, I can't drive. Here we'd sit with the road going from under us, and all the bedroom windows open at home, and all for one miserable nitwit of a scared dog. Can't you come back — you and George? I'll have raincoats and boots ready for you in a minute, and then you and George . . .'

'All right, all right,' the man said. 'Don't get hysterical. If you start bawling too besides those two in the back . . .' He didn't finish, but started the car. He drove slowly, carefully into the blinding rain, hugging the middle of the road. The windscreen wipers could not sweep the rain away fast enough. He held his face close to the windscreen, his jaw set hard.

In the back seat the two children wept hopelessly. 'No, Dad, don't leave him, don't leave him . . . No, Dad,' the girl moaned over and over.

The man glanced briefly at his wife, then back to the road. 'We're coming right back,' he promised the girl woodenly. 'Once we get to the highway we'll really make tracks and get your mother home, and then we'll shoot right back, and I promise you I'll hunt for him till I find him. I know this country.' He peered hard through the windscreen.

'No, Dad. No, Dad,' the girl sobbed. She clung to her brother in her misery. He pushed her away, went on with his own blind, noiseless crying. The girl rocked herself in her absolute helplessness. Suddenly she broke off crying, stared crazily at the car door. She slid forward, reached out her hand to the door.

Her mother caught the movement in the driving-mirror. She flung herself around, made a wild grab for the girl; instead her hand swiped flatly across the girl's face. The girl whimpered and fell back in the seat. 'Well, maybe that'll put some sense in you . . . I didn't mean to hit you. John, she was going to jump out of the car!'

The man said nothing. The woman's shoulders suddenly sagged in an unnerved hunch, her whole body slumped. 'Oh, how that scared me! What a day, and it all started out so fine. If only we hadn't taken that dog along.'

'Never mind that now,' her husband ordered. 'Look,' he said loudly, 'we're coming to the highway, then we'll really get going, and the storm's already letting up a bit – just one of those spring flash storms.'

The boy jerked erect. 'But then if . . .' he stammered. 'But, Dad, then we've got to go right back. Dad, we've got to – not go home first. Can't we, if the storm is over?'

'Yes,' the father said, 'we'll turn around on the cement highway, this road's too narrow, and then we'll go right back. Never mind,' he said sharply to his wife who had not uttered a sound.

'It's all right, John, we'll go back,' she said. She looked at the girl. 'I didn't hurt you, dear? I didn't mean to, I was just trying to grab you in time. Oh, you scared me!'

7. THE NIGHT

When the girl had run from under the bridge, when thunder had crashed and hail had hissed into the creek, the puppy for the first few moments had not noticed. He had not missed the girl. There was that tuft of dried grass swirling down the creek, and to him it looked furry. It was running away from him, and it was furry. He hated it. He was furious and ferocious. He rushed at the creek in little growling rushes. When the tuft of grass swept on he ran after it along the creek beyond the bridge. It was running from him. He barked it on, chased it faster down the creek with

54

his bold barking. Oh, it was scared of him!

Then he became aware that hail was pelting and stinging him. Now he felt it and whimpered and turned. He bowled along on his short legs back to the bridge. The girl was scrambling up the gully. But the girl was making queer scared noises. It scared him, but mutely he tried to follow her the best he knew how. And then he came to the broom lying across his path!

He had not seen the broom when the girl had carried him down in her arms. Now all of a sudden there was the broom. There it lay, and it meant only one thing to him – he had done wrong. Helplessly he stared up after the scrambling, whimpering girl. The rain and hail beating into his little anxious upturned face confirmed it – he had done wrong! The hail stung the way the broom bristles stung when he had done wrong and was being punished. Suddenly there was fierce light and thunder all around him, and he was scared of it, but the broom held him at bay. The broom kept him from following the girl babbling his name in a queer, unknown voice. 'Candy, come on. Candy, come on.'

He could not follow; There was the broom. He crawled a few rubbery steps closer to the broom, but then with a piteous little whimper he flung himself away from it and catapulted under the bridge. He huddled, miserably wet and shivering, under the bridge – waiting. The girl would come, as always she would come and pick him up. He knew. And in her arms there would be no fear of the broom.

She did not come. Instead among the rushing roaring storm noises all about him, above it all, there came their voices – the woman's voice, the big man's voice, the big impatient voices. Oh, he had done terribly wrong this time. But then a little later, there it was – the girl's voice right above the gully. The girl was coming to pick him up. No, she was calling him desperately to come. And desperately he wanted to come, but there was the broom. And then the girl was gone.

Suddenly she was back, but now she was calling him from the other side of the bridge, the other side where there was no broom. He pelted along under the bridge to the other side and waited for her just around the corner of the abutment, just out of the punishing hail and rain, because he knew she was coming. He even caught a brief glimpse of the hem of her coat as she came slithering down, grabbing at a bush to hold herself up. But there she stopped, and the car roared, and the girl screamed, and then she was gone. He tried to follow her. He tried but he couldn't. The bank was too steep, too slippery. The rain gushing down washed his paws from under him; he slid back to the creek bed. He huddled under the bridge.

Once again there was *her* voice, the woman-of-the-broom's voice, screaming at him. And out of the thunder along with her voice came the man's hard bellow. His short, hard, no-nonsense-now voice that had to be obeyed. He had to come, he had done terribly wrong, but he had to come in spite of the broom, for their voices ordered it. He crept from under the bridge. He managed little desperate spurts ahead through the wet slime at each call of his name. And if the man and woman had kept ordering him he might have crawled over the broom, his fear of them overcoming his fear of the broom. But they stopped calling. The car went away.

In the gully the broom slipped from its moorings. He saw the broom twist, and then come sliding down at him. He fled. Behind him the broom swept into the creek, came hurtling on the water. The broom was chasing him! He shrieked in terror as head turned, eyes on the broom behind him, he bowled along on his short legs, hurtling himself along the creek ahead of the broom in the water. The stinging hurt of the rain drove him on still faster. In his mindless terror he confused the pain of hail and rain with the pain from the broom.

The creek had gullied itself deep through the wooded bottoms of the hills. The banks rose sheer. There was no way to get away from the creek. And the broom came on. He ran and ran until suddenly the creek opened into level fields and its banks flattened. He hurtled himself up a low spot in the bank and raced away from the creek and the broom across the flat fields.

When the rain at last eased, the puppy was still running over wide fields far from the creek. His tongue lolled out of his mouth. He swallowed his hot tongue only to loll it out again, but still he ran, not knowing where, almost not knowing why any more. He was running now because he had been running, and because here there was nothing known to him, just wide-open fields and here and there fences and hedgerows. He pulled himself through the fences, pushed through the hedgerows, and ran on again. At the edge of a copse he stumbled into a high pile of stacked firewood. There was room for him between the stacked logs, a deep tunnel-like crevice. He crawled in to its far dark end.

Long after he had crawled into his little tunnel he still lay panting and flattened. His sides heaved, his tongue burned out of his mouth, his lungs seemed on fire. At last he had breath enough to let out a queer little whimper. He was lost. In the midst of his frightened whimpering he fell asleep from exhaustion. He lay as he had crawled under the wood, in the total dead sleep of exhaustion.

When the puppy awoke it was dark under the woodpile, dark in the copse, dark in all the fields. He had slept far into the night; he had heard nothing of the search for him; it had not come near him.

The boy and the girl and their father had slogged for weary hours under the dripping trees along the wandering creek, its banks mired and soggy. They had searched and called his name endlessly. 'Candy, Candy, Candy,' it had sounded endlessly and the echoes over the wooded hills had sounded it back. They had stayed near the creek, since the creek gave some direction to their search. Early spring darkness was coming too soon; there had not seemed to be time enough to continue the search into the fields. Besides there was the mother waiting alone in the car, back on the lonely wooded road under the dark trees. Just knowing she was sitting there hurried their search. Desperately they called towards all the fields. 'Candy, Candy, Candy.'

58

When they had had to end their search the three of them were far from the woodpile where the puppy slept. The three had turned back because darkness was gathering fast. There was nothing left to do but slog wearily back the long way they had come. There was nothing left but the helpless promise of the father. 'It's getting dark, we've got to get back now. Your mother's sitting there alone. But we'll be back the first thing in the morning. Tomorrow's Sunday, and we'll have all day.'

Neither the boy nor the girl said anything; they plodded on behind their father. They didn't cry. Their throats were too dry and tight; they were too tired.

'He's drowned,' the girl told her brother hopelessly.

Her father turned. 'Nonsense,' he said too sharply. 'Even if he did land in the creek, dogs can swim. He'd have swum out here and climbed out into these flat fields. And he's too young to have run very far.'

'He's drowned,' the boy told his father with sombre finality.

'We'll find him,' the man promised unhappily. 'Tomorrow we've got the whole day.'

In the middle of the night the little dog awoke under the woodpile. It was dark, it was cold, it was damp. He awoke beaten. He was bone cold from the penetrating damp that had seeped up from the wet ground into the very marrow of his bones. He shivered and shook. And when he shivered he ached dismally in every sore, stiff joint from his tremendous running of the day before. The darkness and cold and the silence lying all around, the pain throbbing through his whole body, meant only one thing to his puppy mind – punishment for some wrong he had done. He ached, he was cold, he was alone in the dark, therefore he had been punished.

Ah, he was still only a puppy, still with a puppy's

cloudy, baby mind. A little mind that now tumbled all over itself because of his hurt and his pain and his aloneness, the way his little body tumbled all over itself when he was happy and excited with the children. He could not think things out straight, remember things straight. He awoke beaten and guilty, therefore he had done wrong. He awoke aching and hurting, therefore he had been punished. He awoke all alone in the cold and the dark, therefore he had been banished, the way he had always been banished to the cold, dark, lonely cellar when he whined in the night.

He mustn't whine now! He mustn't. He'd be punished still more. But for all that a little whine began rising up out of his throat, as if of itself, and he couldn't stop it. It rose higher, higher, it shrieked out of him – lonely, haunted, lost.

Because he could not stop his shrill whining, he dutifully crawled out to meet his punishment. Painfully he wriggled and backed out from under the woodpile.

He stood outside the woodpile. He whimpered now in real pain and licked at his soreness. All his unused baby muscles seemed to scream with pain. Suddenly he stood still. He looked all around, but he understood nothing of the great night silence around him. The dark trees of the copse loomed over him, the dark night fields stretched dim and silent and endless before him, and he was cold.

He stood there, his little tail whipped tight under his body, stood with his back hunched and rounded and humbled, waiting, ready for more punishment because he was whining in the night. But no one came. No one yelled at him from behind a closed door. There were only the cold night and the silence. Nobody came. And suddenly the little dog's whimper rose to a shriek, but he stood with his little back rounded for punishment.

There was only silence. To that total silence the little dog's mind did not know how to react. If only a twig had fallen. If only something had sounded somewhere. But there was nothing, nothing but the great wide unconcerned night, and his own whining.

He couldn't hold his humble hunched position any longer; he couldn't endure the ache. He had to change his position, and with that change he had to make up his own little mind to do one thing or another, crawl under the woodpile again, or run again. It wasn't that clear in the little dog's mind, but suddenly he was running. The puppy didn't decide it — his body did. He ran. Once he had started to run he ran hard, ran blindly into farther fields, whipped on by the pain in his sore muscles, pursued by the dark and the aloneness and the strange silence of the big fields.

Once he was running he could only run on, senselessly. But his sore muscles limbered and his body warmed, and he was doing something. He was expressing something by his running — what, he did not know. It seemed to mean something, this running ahead — he was going somewhere, somewhere to an end, and to a destiny.

He pulled himself through fences, he crossed roads. But his running only got him farther afield, farther and farther away from the bridge. And at last his running got him to another copse where he stumbled under another woodpile which also had holes into which a puppy could crawl. He crawled in, he slept. He was miles from the bridge. He was in another countryside where the Sunday search by the boy and the girl and their father would never reach him. He was lost.

8. THE STRAY YEAR

In a few short days only one thing remained of the puppy's old life – the guilt feeling, the punished feeling of having done something terribly wrong. For a while there was still the warm feeling for the two children, but it soon became just a vague memory of something that had once been good. All the rest was fear. The fear stayed after his memory of the children, his love for them, had whimpered itself away in the first nights of his whining, homeless wretchedness.

He whimpered softly under the woodpile in the nights. But there were times when he could not seem to help himself. His lost wretchedness would shriek out of him – a haunted, scared dark loneliness. He soon learned to hush his shrieking, for the moment it rose over the wide, silent fields, other dogs began to bark. The ugly threatening barks of the other dogs were telegraphed from house to isolated house; they threatened him from every road, and under the woodpile the puppy would flatten in timid silence. He learned. He learned to keep his whimpering low, lest the other dogs should find him, led on by his crying.

It was not amazing that the little dog so soon forgot the children and his brief home life. In a few short days – just to live, just to keep from starving – his little tumbling puppy mind had to sharpen itself. The puppy had at once to grow into doghood, learn to provide food for himself, learn to avoid danger and threat from the big dogs living all around. The constant hunger and the constant search for food drove everything else out of his mind, everything but the deep feeling of guilt and wrong-doing that had brought him to this misery of starving and loneliness. He even forgot his name.

But what was there that a puppy could catch? Everything in the fields and copses was quicker than he. The terrier in him, the keen sharpening of his sense of smell by hunger, made him smell out mice, but he was too woolly slow to catch them when he found them. They rustled away without his ever catching sight of them, and he would sit whining after them, wistfully begging them to come to him. He couldn't catch a thing. He had to wait for something to die. Wait to find a bird, a rabbit, or even a dead fish stranded along the creek. There was so little that died.

In the early weeks when he still faintly remembered the two children and his home life, when he still might have searched out a house, and might easily have been adopted and taken in because of his puppy innocence and looks, the guarding, barking, threatening dogs kept him away from the houses. The guarding dogs, fulfilling their duty and their purpose, kept him to the back fields far away from people. And in his aloneness in the back fields the fear of people grew. It somehow fitted in with his guilt and his fear. His punishment with the broom had always been associated with big people, and now in his aloneness the fear of grown people became set.

But at night there were no people. At night there were only the dogs. Hunger drove him to the strange dark houses of the strange new countryside. On his stealthy nightly rounds he learned to know the houses that had no dogs, and the houses where the dogs were kept locked inside at night. Even these few houses and the possible crumbs and left-overs in their yards were often denied him by brooms. Nearly always somewhere at a door stood a broom, and to the little dog the fearsome broom was just as effective a means of keeping him away as was a guarding dog. No food smell in the yard could tempt him then; he stole away as stealthily and shadowily as he had come — back to his hidden copse.

The little dog grew up, his mind faster than his under-nourished body. But the rib-rack thinness of his body was right for him in his stray life. It gave him swiftness and elusiveness and a hunted cunning. He was beginning to catch mice. He was learning how to stay in this countryside in spite of other dogs. He was learning how to move about unseen by people.

PART TWO

THE WAY HOME

9. THE CHICKEN

The little stray dog sat in the pine copse far back
in a wild country where no houses were, and no
people. Here he had spent two days in wretched,
hungry uneasiness. Two nights ago when he had made
his regular trip to the yard of the toothless old hound
for his food, Butch was dead – dead and buried. And
there was no food. The little dog had sat on the fresh
dug grave and whined. His whining had betrayed him.
Light had flashed in the house. Then the next day his
helpless whining had betrayed him to the old man
ploughing in the back field – the old man who lived
where the toothless old hound had lived. The little
dog did not remember the old man as the grandfather
of the two children; he knew him only as a threat.
The man had heard his helpless whining, had stooped
and peered. The man perhaps had seen him.

In the sunny day under the pines the little dog
sat and sorrowed. Never had he felt so alone. The
thin helpless whining broke out of his throat again,
it sang around his head, it sang out under the pines,
rose to a high haunted shriek. It went on, miserable,
unloved and lonely. He could not stop it. It was betraying him, again, but it had to go on until all his
misery had drearily sung out of him.

A new restlessness had come to the little dog. He
was desperately hungry after two days of hiding, but
he was too unsure of himself to venture from the pine

copse – he was betraying himself with his helpless whining. In his restlessness the little dog sensed he would have to move on to a new countryside. He sat shivering in the sunniness. He had only this countryside, and now his fear of betraying himself was making him leave that. Now he had nothing. He shivered.

It was hard to leave. But hunger thumped miserably against his ribs. The little dog cried again in a low-pitched voice to himself. Suddenly his whining indecision came to an abrupt end. He snapped his jaws shut. And then he trembled. At that moment it had happened – a chicken had been run over by a car on a distant road. The little dog seemed to sense the warm flesh smell even before his nostrils caught the faint scent.

On the distant, unseen road the chicken flopped mindlessly towards a deep ditch, rolled over into the ditch and lay dead.

The little dog knew it as it happened. He set off like an arrow. He streaked down a wagon lane that cut deep-rutted through wild fields. He kept to the rut. He got to the road swiftly, silently, unseen. There lay the chicken in the ditch.

Before he thought to be afraid or cautious the dog plunged down the ditch bank and seized the chicken to carry it back to the safety of his hidden copse. Wings flapping around his ears, his eyes buried in feathers, he turned to clamber up the ditch bank.

There was a stiff growl from the top of the bank. Everything stopped still in him. He dropped the chicken, stared up blindly, not yet understanding, not quite able to make the quick change from triumph to fear. He made a wild grab as if to retrieve the dropped chicken. In that moment of his indecision the big black dog on top of the bank, wrathful at this defiance by the starved runty creature below him, came hurtling to the bottom of the ditch.

But the little dog had the chicken again, and he had speed. He fled headlong with the chicken down the length of the dry ditch, blindly fastening to the chicken as he ran. The big dog tore silently on behind him. There was another bark and a threatening growl. Another dog appeared at the top of the ditch bank. Now there were scattered barkings along the road. It was a pack, a whole pack of dogs on the road, a whole pack had surprised him at the chicken! They came pelting along the hard level road faster than he could propel himself along the narrow, uneven ditch bottom.

Again a huge dog sailed off the road and hurled himself into the ditch. The little stray dog dropped the chicken, gathered his scared body, and shot ahead. He just eluded the savage leap of the big dog; the dog thudded down behind him; he could feel the thud feathering his back hairs. The two dogs behind him in the ditch came on in concentrated silence. But on the road the barking grew. On the road the pack was gaining on him, was driving alongside him now to get ahead of him in order to wheel and jump in the ditch and cut him off and finish him. How they hated him, the skinny runt, the stranger, the intruder! All their sense of ownership and possession was outraged. They belonged, he didn't belong. They bayed out their hate as they panted down the road to get ahead of him.

The two silent dogs in the ditch came on. They had not even paused for the dropped chicken. The chicken was not now the issue, he was the issue, his unwanted presence in the countryside. They knew him by his scent. That faint elusive scent had been around their barns and houses for a year; they had tracked it through the countryside, but always he had eluded them. Never had he been more to them than a faint, left-behind scent and a distant flash disappearing into the shadows.

Now at last they had him. Here he was fleeing before their noses. The bloodlust started by the chicken was transferred to him. It was in their baying, in their thick, hoarse panting. Still the little dog kept inching ahead of them on the wings of his own terrible terror. Desperately he eyed the field side of the steep ditch, looking for some dip in the bank so that he could hurl himself up and out of the ditch and make for the back fields by way of his secret paths in the hedgerows. There, where he knew every hidden private path, he might still be able to elude the pack.

As if they sensed his desperate plan two dogs at that moment sailed over the ditch and drove on along the field-side bank almost abreast of the little dog at the bottom. Escape to his back fields was cut off by the two dogs. Down in the ditch the little dog still threw himself forward. But it couldn't last. He was tiring. The pack sensed it. The whole pack set up a new baying. Now they had him after a year of never getting close to him. Now they had him. Come on! Come on!

It seemed as if the little dog's brain went still before the knowledge of his coming death – still, and then sharp with a blood-pounding keenness. Suddenly in full speed he threw himself up against the field-side bank of the ditch to lure the pack on the road across the ditch.

It worked. As the little dog jumped up against the ditch bank the whole pack hurled itself over the ditch. The two dogs in the ditch behind him shot up out of it. But as the dog bodies sailed over him high above the ditch, the little dog dropped back to the bottom, then he hurtled himself up the roadside bank and on to the road.

The outwitted pack was thrown off stride. Dogs hesitated, stopped confused, got in each other's way. Then all had to leap the ditch back to the road again, gather speed again.

But now as the pack saw him flash along the road a new baying rushed out of their throats. There he streaked out before them on a level road. Now they had him.

The little dog still ran ahead of the pack, but now he knew the fullness of terror. He was tiring badly. The hard leap out of the ditch had exhausted his last strength. He could not keep up his speed much longer, his throat was burning, his eyes were streaked and bloodshot, he saw only the too-white flashing white-ness of the road directly before him. He was doomed.

Behind him the pack had gone ominously silent as they gained on him. He heard only their hot, hoarse panting.

The mindlessness of terror took over; his little brain stopped functioning. There was nothing left now but his terror speed, but now it was all automatic – just the automatic pistoning of his legs on the hard smooth surface of the road.

But there could be only one outcome, and all his running was just delaying it. The pack was closing in. The pack knew it. The pack came on in a silent, last hard run. Now the little dog's bloodshot eyes saw little any more, he hardly saw the bleached whiteness of the road before him. He was running now only because he had been running. Something would have to happen soon for the little dog, it would have to happen; the little dog could not make things happen any more. He could just run to his end.

And then it happened. Blindly the little dog crashed into something that had come in his way in the middle of the road. He hit it hard. Something moved, thundered up, heaved and pounded. The little dog was thrown back so hard on the rebound of his own speed that he somersaulted, flipped and somehow was on his feet again. But he was stunned.

And then the silent pack was suddenly baying. The pack had closed in. The murderous baying was horrible in his ears; it came from all around him. He could hear the hot, bloody panting under the baying, but still their fangs did not rip him. But now there were strange noises above him – rattlings, banging, then a woman's voice screeched out. A whip cracked. It cracked again. There were vicious whip lashings all around him, but the stunned, blinded little dog sank down in the sand and gravel of the road.

He heard a dog let out a terrible screech. There

were hurt, surprised whimperings among the whole pack, and they didn't close in on him. The whip cracked again. A dog went whimpering down the road, his whimpering fading. Still no hot murderous fangs ripped at the sunken, stunned little dog.

The dog's eyes cleared. His brain, stunned from the crash, came out of its fogginess. And now he realized what had happened. He had run under a wagon! In his blind terror he had run full speed under the back end of a wagon, had run under the whole length of the wagon, and had crashed against the hind legs of the horse. Now he was still under the wagon, for the startled horse had stopped the moment he had hit her.

The moment the wagon had stopped the pack had surged round the wagon to get at him, but the woman on the wagon up above him had turned on the pack and whipped them away. She was still whipping them away. A hurt dog crawled to the roadside. Others, panting and slavering, stood in a confused circle around the wagon just out of reach of the whip's tip. The whip cracked. A terrible shriek cut out of a dog's throat. At that shriek the pack began dribbling off, following the whipped one, who was whimpering and biting at the stinging raw burn of the whip lash along his flank. Slowly, stubbornly, they fell away from the wagon, they all drooped off.

Now only the little dog was left. He lay panting. The woman up on the wagon seat did not know he was there. The woman was talking to the horse. 'Let's get home, Daisy, before that crazy pack of wolves tackles us again. I never saw anything like it – dogs tackling a wagon! What possessed them?'

She clucked to the horse. The wagon wheels started grinding through the sand and gravel. The little dog got up stiffly; he walked along under the wagon, the wagon wheels grinding on either side of him. He walked wearily, head hanging, tongue lolling, but he felt safe. Somehow he sensed that he was safe between the turning wheels. Other dogs could not rush him because of the turning wheels. The hot sun could not reach him.

He walked in the shade under the wagon, he walked silently, while strength and breath ebbed back into his body. He rested as he trudged, so slowly went the wagon. He was not thinking now, not planning, not scheming; he just felt safe and dumb and grateful and spent.

10. THE WAGON

The wagon had rolled a slow quiet mile down the sand and gravel road. Under the wagon the little dog had trudged a slow mile. He padded along. His head still drooped, and he was utterly quiet.

From time to time his ears tensed as the woman up above him on the wagon mumbled things to herself in the hot, quiet afternoon, but he listened to her unafraid. He remembered the whip cracks. This was the woman who had whipped the dog pack away from him. Once when the woman spoke louder to reproach the old horse, the little dog under the wagon waved the tip of his tail.

Later the woman must have fallen asleep, but the old horse trudged along, the little dog trudged along. A half-mile later they came to a little hamlet, five or six houses strung along the road. At one of the houses a dog came barking, then he rushed the wagon as it passed, growling and snarling. The little dog kept

exactly between the two front wagon wheels. The charging dog was frustrated, couldn't solve the puzzle of the turning wheels. He rushed again, but now the turning spokes of the hind wheels held him at bay. He dropped back, barking resentfully. His barking had roused the dogs at every house of the little hamlet. At each house a new dog stood waiting to rush the wagon and the mute little dog under it.

The woman woke up irritated. 'What is it about this wagon?' she screeched at the third barking dog. 'Why must every dog rush at me? You didn't do it this morning when I came through with a load of pigs, and I might have expected it. You get away, beat it, or you'll get the whip, too.' The dog stood his ground, barked back at her. He growled at the little dog under the wagon. The little dog crowded against the hind legs of the horse. The old horse, feeling something touch ing her, promptly stopped and stood stubborn and immovable. She jerked the loose reins and lowered her big head to look past her own legs at the little dog under her. She did not move.

'What is it about these dogs?' the woman screeched. The whip swiped viciously. The farm dog streaked for home. But the old horse looked at the little dog and would not move again in spite of all the woman's cluckings and orders. 'What's under there?' the woman asked the horse. She came clambering down, whip in hand. She came slowly, heavily; she was a huge woman. The little dog moved back under the wagon.

The woman stooped. Then she saw the little dog under the wagon. Whip in hand she peered between the spokes of the wheel at the dog. The dog peered back at her.

'Well, I'll be . . . So it was you under there all the time. So that's why the dogs rush me. Say, that pack chased you under there, didn't they? And now you've got it figured out that they can't get at you under there, so you stayed . . . Well, if that isn't smart! But where do you belong?'

The little dog stared at her between the spokes. The woman was enormous, huge and fat, but she had a friendly voice. The dog's tail almost wanted to wag, but he sat down on it. He stared at her and waited.

'You'd better get for home, Buster,' the woman said. 'If you've got a home.' She waited, but the dog did not move. 'You'd better go. If you stay with this wagon you'll sure be lost, I've got miles to go.'

The little dog sat. The woman shrugged. 'Well, you'd better know – if you want to stay there it's all right with me. But it isn't getting you anywhere.' She looked uncertainly at the mute little dog, then she reached to the wagon seat, pulled down a big black handbag and rummaged in it. She held out a sugar cube in the flat palm of her hand. 'I suppose you like candy?'

74

The dog looked at her gravely. He had a vague feeling that he wanted to wriggle himself closer. 'So you don't like candy? Well, Daisy does.' She walked around to the old horse and fed the piece of sugar to her. Under the wagon the dog's tail waved a little.

Now the woman began the heavy climb back on the wagon. The whole wagon creaked and lurched as she plopped her great weight down on the seat at last. The wagon moved, the little dog got up and walked again.

Beyond the row of houses were open fields with hedgerows and distant wooded hills, but the little dog under the wagon was not even tempted. What he wanted he did not know; why he stayed with the wagon he did not know. Perhaps he sensed that his old haunts were no longer useful to him. Now that the pack had almost had him, they would hunt him down relentlessly in his old countryside. He drooped along, and for the first time in his stray life he was not alert, and not on guard. He felt safe between the wagon wheels. It was wonderful to be slow and poking and half asleep, and safe. In his exhaustion he felt almost too numb to be sharply hungry. He was hungry in a dull, empty way, but he was used to that. The wagon grated along; the woman above him was so quiet she must have gone to sleep again. The old horse was practically sleep-walking.

They plodded on. The horse began to meander from side to side of the road. The dog kept changing directions slowly with the snaking progress of the wagon. The wagon wandered to the roadside where dusty grass grew. The horse jerked the reins out of the sleeping woman's hands, sniffed at the grass, and snorted – it was too dusty for her liking. But down the road a little distance a creek curved briefly towards the road before it meandered across flat fields. Down the bank where the creek ran, the grass grew lush and green. The horse saw it, but she was too shrewd and old to plunge straight down the bank; she took the wagon on a long slow slant along the bank towards the creek. The wagon began tilting. In her sleep the fat woman leaned with the tilting wagon. The wheels still on the top of the bank lifted a moment, but crunched down again. The dog shot from under the wagon.

For a moment the little dog stood bewildered and helpless, then he raced to the old horse, whipped around before her, stood squarely in her path, barking and snarling and showing all his sharp little teeth. He wasn't afraid of the horse, he knew horses. Horses had never chased him in his life in the fields. Horses minded their own business.

The old horse stopped. She stood patiently, indifferent. The moment the wagon stopped the woman awoke 'What's it . . . what,' she stammered. With big sleep-filled eyes she stared down the steep bank from the tilting high seat. It scared her fully awake. She flung herself across the seat to get her weight on the high side of the wagon. The wagon lurched with her movements, but she clutched the whip socket and kept dragging herself across the seat, all the time talking sweetly to the old horse. She got one foot on the roadside wheel. She dropped to the ground. She kept talking nicely to the horse until she could pick up the reins, then she grabbed her by the bridle. 'Back, you, Daisy. Back, back now, just the way you came down. Slowly now, easy does it.' Gradually she worked the horse and wagon back on to the road.

The moment the old horse was back on the road she gave her bridle a savage jerk. She screeched at the horse; she slapped her nose. The old horse rolled her eyes and tried to jerk away, but she held her and yanked her old head until she herself was panting with the effort. The little dog stared at it.

She suddenly dropped her hands. 'There, I guess I lost my head,' she said in a low guilty voice. She was breathless. 'Here, then, here's a piece of candy for you.' She rubbed a sugar cube between the trembling lips of the old horse. 'I ought to give you the whip, but here I'm giving you candy again, because I haven't got any sense. You old goat – you trying to kill me, and I give you sugar!' The horse looked at her meekly and accusingly.

The fat woman drew a deep breath, she looked around at the little dog. 'You're the one that ought to have the candy. I guess if it hadn't been for you I'd have been standing on my head in the creek right now. No more candy, though. I gave that old scalawag, who don't deserve it, the last piece.' She looked at the creek. 'Whew, it's hot,' she said to herself. She went to the creek, pulled a big handkerchief out of the front of her dress and soaked it in the cool creek water. She washed herself with it, her face and neck and down into her dress. The little dog went to the creek and began to lap at the water. The woman studied him. 'Well, can't you be more friendly? Suppose you did save my neck, I saved yours, too, so now we're even. Say! Why don't you go sit in th_ creek? I would if I were a dog.'

As if the little dog understood, he walked into the creek. The cool water soothed his sore, cracked paws. It felt so good his tail began waving. He took quick bites at the water curling around him, and then he sat down in it.

'I'll be blowed,' the woman exclaimed. 'Did you understand me? You must be a bright little fellow. Does it feel good? Well, it gives me a notion.' She clambered up the bank, went to the wagon and pulled a shoe box down from the seat. She returned to the creek, pulled off her shoes and stockings and plopped herself down on the creek bank with her feet in the water. She sat wriggling her toes contentedly, then she opened the shoe box. The dog smelt food; he stood in the creek eyeing the woman and the shoe box but he did not come nearer. 'We're going to eat here,' the woman explained to him. 'Got miles to go yet, but it doesn't matter when I get home. There's nobody waiting for me now that I've got the pigs sold and delivered.'

She peered in the shoe box. 'Pigs!' she exploded. 'It's going to be quiet on the old place until I start a new batch. Hey, this feels good, it's waking me up. It isn't good to sleep in the sun, makes you feel sort of broiled inside and out.' She dug into the shoe box. 'Do you know I've been on the road since three this morning, delivering those pigs? It's slow work with a wagon . . . Ought to get myself a lorry. Hah, that's a good one, me, the pig woman, up in the cab of a lorry.' She laughed until her whole fat body shook.

The little dog in the creek cocked his head, listening to it curiously. The woman held up a sandwich. 'Look,' she said to the dog. 'Food! And you look as if you could stand some. The way some people treat animals! Well, now you can come here and get it – this ought to fetch you, a whole sandwich.'

The dog stood motionless, but at the sight of the sandwich the haunt of hunger seemed to take possession of his whole body. Suddenly he sat down on his haunches in the water, and the eerie, lost cry welled up out of him.

'Here, you stop that!' the startled woman said. 'What's the matter with you? Stop it! It's scary, even if it is in the middle of the afternoon. You stop it.' She threw her sandwich at the dog. He snapped it out of the air, swallowed it in one hard, gorging gulp.

The woman studied him. 'Maybe you're just starved, huh? Starved and timid.' A bitten sandwich came sailing. 'Here, you eat it. You take my hunger away, you looking at me like that and crying – me so fat and you such a bone-rack.'

The wagon on the road creaked. The woman turned. 'Hey, you, Daisy, I wasn't talking to you. You stay on the road – for punishment. Anyway, I haven't any more candy. The candy's all gone.'

'Look at her prick up her sly old ears when I say candy,' she told the dog. 'That's one word she really understands. Hey, you seem to understand it, too! Look at your ears standing up.' She tried it again, watching the dog closely. 'Candy,' she said. 'Candy, Candy.'

In the creek the little dog stood with head cocked to one side, listening to his name. The tip of his tail began to wave uncertainly. 'It's your name,' the woman decided. 'So you must be a city dog. City people give silly names like that to dogs.' All the while she talked she slid herself along the creek bank, closer to him. Now she reached out over the water, holding out a whole sandwich to him. Gradually the little dog stretched towards the sandwich, but his feet stayed planted. When he could almost snap it, the woman drew the sandwich back. He did not follow the sandwich.

'Okay,' she said. 'Okay for you, Candy.' She laid the sandwich next to her. 'It's yours, but here it is and here it stays. You're to come and get it.' There was soft reproach in her voice. She did not look at the dog again, but sat munching a sandwich, leaving her reproach hanging there between them, adding not a single word to it. When she wasn't looking he pulled himself two steps closer. He stopped again, wavered in miserable indecision, unable to tear his haunted eyes away from the sandwich, but he did not come an inch closer.

The woman closed the shoe box, and pulled on her shoes and stockings without a word to the dog. She did not even look at him. She picked up the sandwich and carried it to the horse.

The little dog would have stood meekly by if she had eaten it herself, but now she was holding it out to the horse. His sudden jealous hungry greed was horrible. It stormed in him. He wasn't humble and meek about the horse. He came up out of the creek and raced to the woman. He uttered a short whimper to let her know he was there. He drooled a little.

To his immense relief the woman did not feed the sandwich to the horse. But she did not give it to him either. She went to the wagon with it, laid the sandwich on the seat. He followed her. She turned to him. 'Now if you want it, you've got to let me lift you up on the seat, Candy,' she said quietly. 'It's no sense you walking under that wagon on those pin legs of yours.' Gently talking she took hold of him, and he held himself still. She lifted him quickly to the wagon seat. 'See, nobody is going to murder you . . . and there's your sandwich.'

He was too busy wolfing down the thick sandwich, large chunk by large chunk, to notice the upheaval of the spring seat as the woman clambered up after him. He was too busy scrubbing the seat for the last crumb to be afraid when the woman plopped herself heavily down beside him. The black handbag lay between them; a crumb had got under it; he nosed the handbag aside to get the crumb. The woman clucked to the horse; the wagon lurched into motion. Now there were no more crumbs. The little dog stared down from his great strange height on the moving wagon and became uneasy. The woman noticed. She opened the shoe box, took out a last sandwich and stuffed it in her handbag. She placed the handbag beside her on the seat. It lay between them. 'There,' she said, 'that ought to hold you here and keep you from any crazy notions of jumping down. You'll be all right with me, you'll see.'

11. THE HANDBAG

The long ride on the high wagon seat went on and on because it was so slow. The sun was setting, sun heat mellowed into evening warmth, insects sang. The sing-song and the sleepy jog of the old horse made the little dog unalert and sleepy. The big woman drowsed beside him. The black handbag still lay between them, separating them a little. Now the dog settled his head on the bulging handbag as if it were a pillow. He blinked his eyes towards sleep only to open them wide again in little scares and alarms. Then he slept. The horse lumbered on, the slow wheels ground in the gravel.

Later the horse jerked her head away from a buzzing insect. The jerk pulled the reins out of the sleeping woman's hands. Immediately the old horse knew it. Immediately the horse headed for the roadside, studied and sniffed the roadside grass, snorted at its dustiness. The wagon meandered to the other side of the road.

Ahead on the road the old horse smelled green, fresh clover. It grew below the high road bank, screened from road dust by a clump of elderberry bushes. The horse went straight for the clover. Behind her the wagon rode into the elderberry bushes. It gave one sickening lurch. In that swift, sudden jolt woman and dog were pitched off the tilting seat down to the flat marshy land below the road bank. The old horse, feeling the shafts twisting against her flanks, feeling the wagon tossing behind her, took one scared clumsy leap down the bank. Miraculously the empty wagon pulled free from the bush clump, straightened, fell back on all four wheels. The old horse went with it to the clover patch.

Down below the bank in deep marsh grass a bewildered little dog got woodenly to his feet. A yard away from him lay the big woman, legs sprawled, arms flung out, face down in the grass, motionless. The old horse grazed in the clover. The dog looked at the wagon moving away. He looked at the woman again. He started to go to her as if to nudge her. But when he got to her he didn't quite dare. He backed away from her. He stood looking helplessly from the wagon to the woman, and then he saw the big black handbag that had been flung beyond the fence that stretched along the marshy field.

The wagon was moving away again with the grazing horse. The dog stared at the woman, and then he backed still farther away from her. He backed into the fence. He turned as if to go through the fence and run away across the marshy field. But there lay the purse. He pulled himself through the fence, he sniffed at the handbag, and then he lay down behind it. He sank down in the marsh grass, stretched his head on his paws, and over the purse he stared unblinking through the fence at the woman.

A car passed but in the mists over the marsh no one in the car saw the woman and the dog, did not even see the horse and wagon behind the screen of elderberry bushes. The rush of the car on the high road scattered the mist for a moment, but then the mist gathered again and spread like a thin grey sheet above the marshy field and the woman and the dog. Now the horse had finished with the patch of clover, and dragged the wagon farther away. The dog lifted his head at the sound.

Later the wagon wheels crunched and grated on gravel. The horse had gone back to the road; the wagon wheels in the gravel began turning with a quicker urgent sound. The hooves of the horse pounded. The horse was going home. She had found no more clover, it was late, and now she was eager for her stable. The wagon sounds faded, then merged with the frog sounds in the marsh and the evening insect sounds. Then they were gone.

A stillness seemed to settle down over the near field where the woman lay and the dog sat watch over the handbag. It seemed to sift down with the floating mists. The little dog sat listening again for the wagon sounds. There wasn't a sound. And suddenly he lifted his mournful head towards the blankets of mist rolling above him and out of his throat ripped the lost, haunted cry. It went on and on, shrill, piercing, miserable. It rose higher and higher.

Later the dog's ears picked up the sound of a car coming slowly down the road. He did not stop his whining. Down the road the car stopped, the motor sounds died, the car had parked.

In the car at the edge of the road a young man and a girl sat close together looking out at the peaceful night fields. Suddenly the girl jerked away, sat erect. 'Fred, I hear crying in that marsh. Listen to it, it's awful!'

The young man leaned forward, listened. Then he laughed away her alarms. 'It's just a dog howling somewhere.'

'You're just saying that. . . . Listen, that isn't a dog, that's . . . It . . . it isn't human. Fred, let's get away from here!'

Fred laughed. 'It's only a dog,' he said, boyishly scornful of her alarm. 'Dogs do that sometimes – just sit and howl for no good reason. It sounds spooky, but it doesn't mean a thing. Maybe he's just lost or hungry.'

'It's supposed to mean that somebody has just died or is going to die,' the girl stated stubbornly. She shivered. 'Fred, I'm scared!'

The young man shrugged elaborately and started the car. 'It's down the road a little way. You'll see, it's just a dog.' The car bumped slowly along. The little dog heard it coming. He stopped his tormented keening, sat listening tensely.

'I don't hear it now,' the girl said, her ear close to her tightly shut window. 'It's gone now.' The car dragged to a slow stop. The boy shut off the engine again. 'It's nice here,' he said, but the girl stayed huddled against her door, head tilted, listening.

Suddenly down the bank it began again, and now it was directly opposite the car. 'There he is,' Fred said. 'Just a little dog. He's right below my window here.' He wound the window down, pulled the girl towards his window so she could see it was only a little dog. 'See him? That's all it is, just a little dog . . . What's the matter, Rover?' he called through the open window. 'You lost or something?'

The girl leaned over him, peering. Suddenly she grabbed the boy's arm. 'Fred, what's that in the grass? No, right under the bank, closer than the dog. Fred! Somebody did die!'

He thrust her away, stuck his head out of the window. 'It's a woman!' He had the door open, but the girl grabbed him and pulled him back. 'Don't you dare go down there and leave me here alone. She's dead! Fred, if you go down there I . . . I'll never speak to you again.'

The girl's hysteria unnerved the boy. He looked at her, looked uncertainly at the dark form below the bank. 'Maybe we ought to go to the first farmhouse and call the police,' he said uncertainly.

'Yes, yes, let's get out of here,' the girl pleaded. She started crying.

'But we can't let her lie there! She's face down in the grass, she'll choke, and it takes time for the police and the ambulance. . . .' He had summoned up all his courage, he had the door open and one foot on the running-board. The girl attempted to drag him back. 'Fred, if you leave me here, I'll never go out with you again,' she threatened helplessly.

'Margie, be your age!'

He jerked away from her, felt his way down the

misty bank. The little dog stared up at him, waited.

The boy stooped gingerly over the silent, sprawled woman. He touched her arm, quickly drew his hand back. 'She's out cold,' he shouted up the bank.

The girl in the car went on with her hopeless crying, didn't listen.

Now that the sprawled woman remained lying still, the boy got up a little more courage. He took her head and turned it so her face would be out of the grass. Then he knelt over her irresolutely. He helplessly pulled a few handfuls of thick marsh grass away from in front of her mouth. He felt her cheek with the back of his hand. He stood up, stared around, looked at the silent dog without seeing him. He scrambled up the bank and back to the car.

The car drove away fast. The little dog settled down on the handbag, lay silently staring at the blank, white face of the woman now that it was turned towards him. Later the road filled with noises. A car came roaring up, doors slammed, four men plunged down the bank. Their voices and their talk were all around the woman. The boy, Fred, was with them.

They milled around, talking, peering, paying attention only to the woman, hardly noticing the quiet little dog beyond the fence. The dog just stared, but he didn't take flight. For some reason he stayed with the handbag.

Now down the road came flashing lights and the shrieking of sirens. A police car came rushing down on them, followed closely by an ambulance. Behind the ambulance came a stream of cars. Brakes shrieked on the road, car doors slammed, people gathered in dark clusters above the bank. Now a sharp spotlight shone down the bank. 'Look!' a woman's voice shrilled from the road. 'Why, look, there's a little dog, and he's guarding her handbag . . . Ah.'

In spite of the noise and the voices and the people, the little dog stayed loyal to the handbag for some dim reasons of his own. Maybe it was only because of the food smell that came seeping out of the handbag from the sandwich inside it. Maybe it was instinct, the same instinct that had made him in his puppy days drag sweaters to his tiny corner between the gas stove and the wall. Whatever it was, it also helped that no one paid attention to him in the total concern for the woman. Now they came down the bank with a stretcher. They strained at lifting her. 'Weighs a ton,' somebody grunted. 'What a place for her to pick. We'll never get her up that bank.'

They walked away along the fence with the woman on the stretcher, looking for a spot where the bank might be less steep. The ambulance on the road slowly backed with them. The whole crowd followed, curious to see the hoisting of the stretcher with the motionless woman on it. The little dog alone stayed behind with the handbag. He lay quiet, watchful.

A man in uniform came back along the fence – alone. He squatted down on the other side of the fence before the dog. 'Now may I have that handbag, little fellow?' he said in a calm, casual voice. The fence was between them; the little dog did not move.

'You're a good dog, guarding it like that, but now I've got to take it along. You can come, too,' the man explained softly. He slowly stretched his hand through the fence, was reassured when the dog did not growl or bare his teeth. But neither did the little dog retreat – the fence was between them. By leaning hard against the woven wire the officer could just reach the hand-bag strap. He dragged the handbag from under the dog, his eyes alert for any movement. The little dog meekly let the handbag be dragged away, but saw to it that he stayed out of reach himself.

The policeman had the handbag through the fence; he opened it and flashed a light into it. 'For identification,' he muttered to the dog. 'My gosh, a sandwich! Even kept food in here – well, it's almost a suitcase.' Then after peering at some papers he had pulled out of the purse, he unwrapped the sandwich and held it through the fence for the little dog. The dog stared steadfastly at the sandwich, but did not move an inch. Suddenly, as if by accident, the man dropped it. The little dog shot forward to grab it, but as he seized the sandwich, the man's hand closed over his neck. 'Sure, you just hang on to your sandwich, it's yours,' the policeman said soothingly, 'but you've got to come with me. Don't lose the sandwich now, but here you come.' He dragged the little dog through the fence. The dog made no struggle, just let himself be dragged, but his jaws stayed closed on the sandwich. 'Sure, you just hang on to it,' the man said. 'You're going to need a lot of sandwiches to get you into some shape.'

The policeman, continuing to talk, carried the little unresisting dog to the police car, and slid into the seat. There was another uniformed man sitting behind the wheel. Without a warning the car shot out from the side of the road, the siren began shrieking. The awful, close, piercing shriek unnerved the little dog. He dropped his sandwich. In one wild leap he was out of the policeman's arms, and over his shoulder. He thudded to the floor behind the seat. He cowered there, terrified.

'Better cut out the siren,' the policeman told his partner, 'it scares him silly. Queer little scared creature to stay with that handbag.' He picked up the sandwich and dropped it to the little dog. 'Here, fellow, maybe this will make you feel better.' But the little dog did not move.

Later the police car came out of country darkness

and entered the town. The little dog on the floor was aware of continuous light, continuous flashing and the constant roar and rumble of many sounds coming at him from every direction. Uneasily he looked up from the floor at the window, confused by the strangeness of light in the night. The sandwich lay before him.

The car stopped at last before a huge building. Now the uniformed man stooped over the back of the seat and pulled him up from the floor. The dog did not resist, just let himself be taken.

The policemen took the dog into the hospital. They took him into a room that was one white glare of light. The whole room bustled with white-coated men and white-skirted women. The little dog stared mutely at it all, held himself deathly still so as not to be noticed. Then suddenly he was peering from the policeman's arm down into the blank white face of the big woman. She was lying on a table. She lay still. The dog stared at the woman, his scared eyes big and fixed.

'He doesn't give the slightest sign of recognizing her,' the man who held him said to his partner.

Now a white-coated man stooped over the woman.

'How long before she comes to, Doc?' the policeman said. 'We've got to know about her and about this dog – whether it's hers and what she wants done with him.'

The doctor glanced up, then was busy again. 'It's hard to tell,' he said, 'but I doubt whether she'll know or care what's to be done with the dog . . . Maybe in the morning.'

The policemen took the little dog back to the car. The car rushed down lighted streets again. The little dog stared. There was no silence, no hiding, no safety of darkness anywhere – all was light and flashings, and noise. It was dizzying. There was no hiding from it.

The car stopped again, this time before a small

building. The policemen took him into a little room where there was nothing but one dim light and an old man. They talked. Then the old man got up and the policemen followed him with the dog. The old man snapped a button, opened a door, and suddenly they were in a room with nothing but dogs. It was a madhouse of dogs. With the lighting of the room and the entry of the men the room seemed to explode with barking dogs. Dogs were everywhere, against every wall, in wire cages tier on tier. Everything rattled as dogs banged and leaped against their wire cages. The little dog cringed in the policeman's arms.

The chase by the pack was too recent. Now after his life-long fear of dogs, he was surrounded by dogs. The old man opened a cage. The policeman shoved the dog in the cage. The door banged shut. The little dog immediately knew he was caged, and he immediately surrendered. He crawled into the farthest corner of his cage, flattened himself and lay still. All around him wild barking surged and bounded and exploded through the tile-walled room.

'Got something to eat for him?' the one policeman said. 'I know it's after hours, but he's starved.'

'All the others would go nuts,' the old man said. 'It would be a madhouse all right. We'd better get out of here and turn the lights out or they won't settle down for hours.'

The three men went away. The little dog stayed pressed against the rear of his cage, but there was no hiding anywhere. All was open wire, except the tiled back wall. He pressed against the wall, trying by his stillness to become unseen by the other dogs. He closed his eyes to shut them out.

Outside the policeman's car drove away. In the room the wild, mixed barking gradually ebbed away. Gradually the little dog began to sense that the other dogs were not interested in him. He opened his eyes. He stared across a narrow aisle into a cage where sat a flattened, terrified cat. The cat stared back at him, her eyes wide with pain and fear. And then the lights went out.

12. THE DOGS' HOME

The din in the dogs' home was back in the morning. It came back with the light. Gradually as daylight grew in the cool, shiny-tiled room the restlessness grew. The time for their food was nearing, and the dogs knew it. In all the wire cages dogs started pacing back and forth.

Occasionally the watchful restlessness would explode into flurries of questioning, impatient barks. Then there would be a lull as the whole room listened for the first sound that indicated the old caretaker was coming with the food. A single short bark by any one dog would start them off again. It grew and grew into a tumult of wild barking. It crashed against the walls. If only they had barked together, but it was all intermingled, hard, furious, senseless. The noise was painful to the little dog's ears after the field silences of his stray life, and his own secretive silence. The poor lone cat sat petrified.

At last the door opened. The old man came in pushing a cart with food in front of him. Pandemonium broke loose, the barking rose to a wild roar, dogs threw themselves against the rattling wire doors. The old man stopped in the doorway. 'Quiet!' he yelled at the roomful. 'Quiet, or you'll get nothing. Nothing!' There was one moment of absolute silence. It couldn't last. The banging and the barking broke out again as the man advanced into the room. 'Quiet!' he yelled uselessly. 'Quiet! I can't stand it, I tell you. I can't stand it.' He began throwing the food into the cages as fast as he could to put an end to the noise. After all the others were fed he came back to the cat and the little stray dog.

The old man talked in soft fretful tones to the little dog and the cat. First to the cat. The cat had not eaten yesterday, and there was reproach in the old man's voice. The cat did not seem to have moved or stirred all during the night. It still sat huddled against the cold tile wall at the back of its cage. It did not respond to the kindness in the old man's voice. It asked nothing, expected nothing – just lived in a perpetual anguish among the dog noises.

The old man tried to tempt it with a bit of fish; the cat did not stir. The old man took the cat's untouched meal of the day before and pushed it into the little dog's cage. 'You deserve it, little fellow, you're quiet. It isn't that the cat would eat it anyway. I'm not exactly taking candy from a baby,' he explained. 'But you just eat hearty, and if you're not getting enough, you just say so.'

The old man laughed at his own words. He tried to draw the cat into the conversation. He kept turning his head and talking to her. The cat would not be drawn. The old man's voice fretted and worried about the cat as he talked to the little dog. 'I'd take you home with me, both of you. You just for the sheer wonder of having a quiet dog, and the cat because it's being tortured to death by the barking. But I'm with dogs all day long, I've just got to get away from animals at night. I can't stand it, I tell you. Anyway, you belong to somebody. And I don't like cats, I think . . .'

The old man was kindness. No matter how much he yelled at the roomful of dogs – he was kindness. In the few days of his stay, the little dog began to look for the coming of the old man. Just for his coming, with food or with empty hands, just so he came with his soft, worried voice. He was kindness. Even the cat now slightly turned her head when the old man came through the door.

In between the visits of the old man the little dog and cat sat staring at each other across the narrow aisle. But sometimes the little dog napped. He had learned to sleep among all the yapping and the barking and the crashing of the wire cages. The cat never napped. The cat didn't sleep, didn't eat, wanted to die, and was dying slowly with the tough patience of a cat.

There were visiting hours when people came with

the clean smell of the outdoors on their clothes. They paced along the cages, peering in, talking as they moved from one cage to the next. Often there were children with the grown-ups. Sometimes there was a reunion – a dog in a cage suddenly going mad with joy, not able to contain it, bursting with it. Then would come the happy cry of the people, the excited squeal of children as they found their lost dog. The cage would be opened, down in the aisle would be a dog crazily leaping up at his people, shaking himself to pieces with his wagging. They would go, and the cage would stand empty. But always the cage filled again. Soon new barkings would come out of it, sharper or hoarser than the barkings of the former dog.

Nobody came for the little dog. Nobody came for the cat, except that now the old attendant took the cat away for an hour or so a day.

The fourth day a little girl came all alone. Timidly she sidled along the cages, clutching the hand of the old attendant. She did not say a word even though the old man was friendly and chatty. He led her twice around both sides of the room. He stopped at the little dog's cage, lifted the little girl. 'Now if I could give him away, that I'd say would be the dog for you – a quiet little dog for a quiet little girl. But he belongs to a lady in a hospital so I mayn't give him away.'

The round face of the little girl peered at him through the trellis work of the wiring. The little dog peered back. For the first time in many days an urge came to him to wag his tail – a soft little girl, and faintly perhaps he remembered.

The little girl looked at the little dog. 'I don't want him,' she said softly. 'I want the cat.'

The old attendant almost dropped her. He had the cat's cage open, he placed the cat in the little girl's

94

arms. She hugged the cat to her. And then they were gone.

In a few moments the old man was back. He stood rubbing his hands excitedly before the little dog's cage. 'She took the cat,' he explained. 'She took the cat.' He excitedly took the last dish of food from the cat's empty cage and pushed it into the little dog's cage. 'It'll be a week before the barking goes out of that poor cat's ears. I know. Even on my vacations it's a week before it goes out of my ears – but then she'll start to live again. Just the same I had her lapping a couple of tonguefuls of milk in my office today,' he proudly told the little dog. 'I'd have found a way. But now she's home.'

The little dog peered at his happiness. The old man who was kindness was happy, his voice did not fret. The urge that had come with the little girl to wave his tail, now came with the old man. But there was the cat's food – boiled kidney. The little dog ate as the old man talked.

The old man was gone when the dog had finished with the kidney. But in his cage the dog wagged his tail in memory of the kidney, and of the good man who was kindness and who had been happy. The cat's cage was empty.

The day the cat left, they came for the little dog – the same two blue-coated policemen. They stood before the cage with the old attendant. They were looking him over. The little dog looked at them. He did not feel unfriendly towards them, and he did not feel afraid.

'George, how'd you do it in just four days? He's filling out.'

The old attendant beamed, but his voice was worried. 'I tell you it's a shame. If that fat woman won't feed him, don't give him back to her, bring him here. Another week and I'd have made him look like something. I tell you, I'd have made him human.'

The two policemen laughed. 'Never heard you wanting a dog back before – haven't you got enough dogs?'

'Do you know he never once barked?' the old man told them earnestly. 'If that woman doesn't want him, I'll take him for myself, I'll take him home. He's different, he's quiet, and I can talk to him.'

The policemen took him away.

Once more the little dog was in the police car with the two officers, but now it was day-time, and the little dog stared blankly at the crowded streets, the rushing cars, the scurrying people, and the huge stores of the downtown section. He did not understand it, but it did not seem quite so terrifying now, not after the four days in the ear-deafening dog pound.

The police car swept up the drive to the same hospital again. This time the two officers took the little dog into an elevator, and then down long corridors. They passed many doors, but at last they went through two double doors that swung shut behind them. The policemen swept their caps off their heads. They were in a long ward. The two men walked awkwardly and self-consciously down the long aisle between two rows of women on white pillows in white beds. The policemen marched up to a bed and stood uncomfortably beside it. All the faces on all the white pillows were turned to them and the little dog. Only the fat woman lay with her eyes shut. The little dog stared down on the big round face of the woman. He held himself very still. Everything was strange here, even the fat woman was strange, with a strange, white, still face.

The policeman cleared his throat. 'This was the little dog we found with you, Ma'am. He was guarding your handbag.'

The woman roused. 'Oh,' she said startled. Her eyes flashed big when she saw the two policemen beside her bed. 'Oh, what's happened now?' She did not seem to notice the little dog.

The policeman began again. 'We found this dog with you, guarding your handbag, and now that you're out of danger, we've come to find out if he's yours, and what you want done with him while you're in the hospital.'

'Dog?' she said. She shook her head, frowned. 'I haven't any dog, just an old horse and some pigs. Oh, no, I sold those . . .'

The policeman took the little dog and held him out above her. 'This dog,' he said very slowly, as if talking to an idiot, 'was found where you had been thrown. He was guarding your handbag . . .'

'My handbag? Where is my handbag? It had all the money for the load of pigs!' The woman tried to sit up; she looked wildly about her; she even felt the bedding around her. 'My handbag.'

'Don't worry, your handbag is in the safe at police headquarters. The money's all there – it'll be returned to you intact . . . But now about this little dog?'

'Oh, don't bother me with a dog. I'm only just coming to my senses again – if I ever had any. I don't want a dog.' She closed her eyes.

The policemen looked at each other and shrugged. Abruptly they turned and walked stiffly from the room, feeling all the eyes following them. 'Hey,' the fat woman suddenly yelled. 'Hey, what's the matter with me? Come back here.'

The policemen turned. The woman was sitting up in bed, a corner of a blanket tossed over one shoulder. It was her old voice. The little dog looked at her; the tip of his tail began to wave. The policemen carried him back. The big woman looked up at him. 'Candy, wasn't it?' she said softly. 'Didn't we decide your name was Candy? Hi, Candy.' His whole tail waved.

'So he is yours,' the policeman said above him.

The woman shook her head. 'No, I think he's a stray. I picked him up because a pack of farm dogs were closing in on him. Let's see, yes, I had him on the seat, I was going to take him home with me. He must have pitched off the wagon with me. So he guarded my handbag? Well, Candy . . . You took care of the old horse, didn't you?' she suddenly asked the policemen.

'What horse? There was nothing along that road but you and the dog . . .'

'Then she went home, the old scoundrel. Left me there for dead and went home. But it's just like her. How long have I been here?'

'Four days.'

She pursed her mouth as if to whistle. 'Then Daisy's been home alone four days, with nobody to take care of her. Not that she won't manage for herself! By now she's no doubt broken up the wagon. But it's a good thing I sold all the pigs – four days, by now they'd be eating each other . . . But could you take care of the old horse for me? But watch her – she's an old devil.'

'We'll take care of it – go there directly. But what about . . . about Candy here?'

'Oh, Candy. He isn't really mine, you know, but I *was* going to take him home with me. He was such a sorry, beaten little thing. And he's bright!'

'Okay, then, we'll keep him at the dog's home until you're ready to leave here. That is, if you still want him. We've found a good home for him already, so if you don't want him, you see you don't have to take him.'

'Look, he stuck with me when I landed on my fat

head, what do you think?'

The policemen grinned. 'You've got something there. If it hadn't been for his howling, you might still be in that marsh.'

'He'll get good care in that dogs' home while I'm here?'

'The best. If there's anybody that would be kinder to little Candy here than you, it'd be old George at the dogs' home. In fact, he's the man that wants him.'

'Well, he can't have him, but tell him to feed him extra. I'll pay for it. And George gets a whole slab of smoked bacon from me, tell him. And so does each one of you if you take care of old Daisy for me. You can farm her out at one of the neighbours'.'

She slid under the covers, pale and tired, and closed her eyes. 'I'm not much yet, I guess,' she whispered. 'You, Candy, you fatten up, but good, hear? You're my dog now – and you and I have got to sort of match.'

13. THE CHILDREN'S WARD

At the end of the long corridor the two policemen stood waiting with the little dog for the hospital lift.

'He wasn't too excited about the pig woman, was he?' One of the policemen studied the little dog as the other held him. His big face came close. 'Hey, Candy, you're not a bit friendly. You're just quiet all the time. You're not even friendly with us. You're just a mouse. Say, isn't that lift ever coming? What do you think, do we take the dog along to the pig farm? We've got to see about that horse, you know.'

The man with the little dog in his arms shook his

head. 'Nope, if he got away from us in the country, he'd be gone, because that's all he knows. No, right back to old George he goes, safe in a cage. George will win him over if anybody can. Hey! That lift isn't going to come! Let's walk down. Okay with you, Candy? Anything's okay with you, isn't it? Someday you ought to bite somebody. It would do you good.'

The two men chuckled as they walked down the stairway, but the little dog hardly seemed aware of them. Down below him stretched the corridor of the next floor. Down that corridor a janitor came backing out of a supply room with an armload of mops and brooms. The little dog stared at the brooms. He began to tremble. He tried to squirm out of the policeman's hold. The policeman placed a big restraining hand over his back. 'Hey, what's the matter? What's scaring you?'

Now the janitor hurried away down the corridor with his awkward armful. The little dog relaxed a little, but kept a watchful eye on him. The janitor walked faster and faster to keep control over his unbalanced load. The two policemen came slowly on behind. Down the corridor the janitor made a frantic grab for a mop that was slipping from his hold. Two brooms got away from him as he grabbed the mop; they clattered to the floor. The man stood with raised knee balancing his load while he tried to pick up the fallen brooms.

'Go ahead, we'll get them,' one of the policemen yelled at him.

'Thanks.' The janitor arranged his load and walked on, leaving the two fallen brooms sprawled across the corridor. Each policeman stooped to pick up a broom, but as the man that held him leaned over, the little dog went berserk. He pawed and struggled to fight himself free and get away from the broom. The man made a grab for him. The little dog bit at him in blind terror. Then he was free. He hurtled over the man's shoulder, plunged to the floor and hurled himself down the long corridor.

'Stop him, stop him!' the policeman yelled to the janitor. 'Stop that dog.'

The man whirled. The little dog saw him come with the brooms. With a yelp he flung himself away, pelted down the hall again towards the two policemen. The amazed men stood there, the brooms they'd picked up still in their hands. But one of them suddenly stuck out his broom to keep the dog from charging past them. The little dog slithered to a desperate halt. Now his escape was cut off by brooms. He turned, but behind him came the janitor with all the brooms. The little dog backed against the corridor wall, facing all of them, teeth bared in terror. He snarled and snarled, but his tail was plastered between his legs.

'Look at that, look at that,' the one policeman said. 'Did you say a mouse? He's vicious.'

'No, he's scared down to the bone. It must be the brooms.' The policeman who had carried him set his broom against the wall, then came a few steps towards the little dog, and squatted down in the middle of the hall. 'Candy,' he said. 'Candy, you come here. Here, Candy.'

Slowly, the little dog began to obey. He seemed to have to pull himself towards the man against his own will. He dragged himself over the floor, his sharp little teeth still bared, but he was in abject fear.

'Take my broom and walk around the corner with both of them,' the policeman ordered his partner. 'Now, Candy,' he said softly. 'Now it's only you and me. You see, I have no brooms – the brooms are gone. And, Candy, you're a good dog, a very good dog.'

The little dog still dragged himself towards the man,

but his agonized eyes didn't even begin to believe the man's words. Down the hall the janitor had once more rearranged his sprawling load of brooms and mops. He stood for a moment looking at the crawling dog, but his load was heavy, and he called to the farther policeman. 'If you could bring me those two brooms now, I think I can make it in one trip.'

The little dog was moving towards the hunched policeman. Then suddenly he saw the other policeman come striding towards him with the brooms. He cowered back. Then the policeman passed with the two brooms. In that moment the little dog shot forward between the two policemen and hurtled away down the corridor.

The hunched policeman jumped to his feet. 'That was a daft thing to do,' he savagely told his partner, 'It's brooms he's scared of, so scared that we may never get him back now.'

In the brief moment he'd turned to berate his companion, the policeman had lost sight of the little dog. When he turned to look again the dog had disappeared. On heavy feet, trying at the same time to be somewhat quiet in a hospital, the two men took after him. At the end of the corridor another corridor angled to the left; to the right was a stairway leading down to the next floor.

'He turned towards the stairs,' the janitor yelled.

The policemen clattered down the stairway. But the floor below was the same maze of corridors. The policemen ran down the main corridor. 'Just so he doesn't find the next stairway down to the main floor. Because if he finds an outside door open, we've seen the last of him.'

'I was just trying to be a pal and help out the janitor,' his partner tried to explain.

'Yes, I know. You go down to the main floor.

I'll cover this one,' he ordered his partner as he walked away. Various short corridors branched off the main corridor, but nowhere did the searching policeman see any sign of the dog. Suddenly he heard sounds coming from a far corridor—high voices, laughter.

He rounded a corner. There at the end of a short corridor were double doors with the lettering on the glass: CHILDREN'S WARD. One of the doors stood open. From the ward came the high, excited sounds. The policeman burst into the ward. The whole ward was bedlam. Children were standing up in their beds in their excitement. Many were running around the beds, chasing something—yelling, squealing, laughing.

A little girl near the door, hopping up and down in her bed in spite of a bandage across one eye, suddenly saw the policeman. 'Ooh,' she shrieked, 'a little dog just came in here. Oh, he's scared and funny, he just tears all over and runs into things. We're all trying to catch him, but I mayn't get out of bed. And nurse is after him with a broom.'

'With a broom!' the policeman exploded. 'That's all we needed.' He sprinted forward.

In the far corner of the long ward behind a bed a nurse rose tall among a clamouring ring of children. They hopped up and down around her in their excitement. The nurse suddenly leaned forward, began making savage thrusts with a broom. Above the voices of the children rose the terrifying yelpings of the little dog.

'Look at him bite that broom! Look at him. Oh, he's mad!'

The cornered dog's snarling attack on the broom scared the nurse. She backed away into the crowd of children, tried to shove the children back. 'Everybody back in bed. Get in your beds! That dog is mad! Get in your beds where you'll be safe.'

The children were too excited to obey. Hysterically the nurse gripped the broom and raised it. 'I'll get you out of there,' she screamed.

'Let me through, please!' the policeman pleaded behind the children. He hesitated, eyed his heavy shoes among all the bare toes. But then he leaned far out over the children, reached out and grabbed the upraised broom. The nurse whirled. 'What . . . Oh!' she gasped when she saw the policeman. 'Help me get that dog out of here – he's mad, and here of all places!'

'He's all right,' the policeman told the frightened woman. 'He's just scared of your broom.' He tried to pull the broom out of the woman's hysterical grasp.

She let go of the broom, grateful for the presence of a man, a uniform. All the children stared wide-eyed at the big policeman who had appeared so suddenly. The uniform cowed them. They guiltily began to sidle off to their beds. The corner had almost emptied when a boy came sliding on his stomach from under one of the beds with the little dog grasped in his hands. The little dog did not snarl now, just held himself still. The boy rose up from the floor with the dog. 'I got him, I got him,' he yelled to all the ward. 'Look, I got him.'

'Oh, look, Jerry's got him!'

The fear of the policeman, everything was forgotten. From the whole ward they came streaming out of their beds again. Only four or five forlorn little figures stayed in bed, raising themselves, clutching the covers in their excitement. The others crowded around the boy with the dog hugged in his arms. 'Why, he's a good little dog! Oh, he's a good little dog. He isn't mad . . . Let me pet him, too. Let me . . . Please, you already had your turn . . .'

The dog was not afraid of the children. He let himself be held, let himself be petted. But his watchful eyes were guardedly on the nurse, the woman who had wielded the terrible broom. Now the nurse pushed among the children. 'All right, now this is enough. Now give me that dog, and everybody back to bed.' The children were reluctant to obey, hated being pushed away from the dog.

The nurse looked appealingly at the policeman. 'This is awful, they shouldn't be out of their beds, and all excited. . . . Jerry, you give me the dog,' she ordered the boy. 'Now, this minute.'

The boy backed away from her into the corner. 'You know a dog can't be here,' the nurse said to the boy. 'Now are you giving him to me, or must I get the broom?' She reached out, picked up the broom leaning against the wall where the policeman had set it.

Before her threat of the broom the boy sullenly backed against the wall, then stooped, and set the little dog free. The dog shot away under the beds. The policeman hurried down the ward, trying to keep his eyes on the dog, but the children kept getting in his way. At the door the little one-eyed girl was eagerly waiting for him. 'If you catch him, may I pet him too? I never even petted him, so will you bring him back and let me pet him too?'

'Bring him back?'

'Yes, he went down the hall. He was such a nice dog, too, and he wasn't a bit mad when Jerry held him.'

The policeman muttered something and was out the door. There was no sign of the little dog.

14. THE CAPTAIN

The little dog plunged down a stairway to the main floor of the hospital. At the end of the corridor an outer door suddenly opened as a man came in. The little dog shot through the doorway as the door closed behind the man.

The dog tore across the spacious lawns of the hospital, and down the first street he came to. An urge was in him, a terrible need to get far away from the building and its brooms. It was all back, the terror, the way it had been in his puppy days when the woman in the clean house had come for him with a broom. Now after a full year it had happened again, and it was as terrifying as it had always been.

Out of old habit the little dog used clumps of bushes and hedges to screen his movements. He ran surely, he ran fast, for he knew where he was going – the only place he wanted to go. There was only one place for him – back to the little building with the many dogs. Back to the old man who was kindness. There was food, and there was safety in a cage. As his terror seeped out of him the new urge took hold – to go back to the man who was kindness. It was almost like a hunger, so sharp and urgent did it become.

His instincts took over, his hounded wits became keen and sharp again. He stopped briefly in a shaded yard, lifted his nose, sniffing, sensing out the way to the dog pound. And then he knew, and then he started.

He ran steadily in a little gangling sideways run that attracted no attention to him but got him down the streets at swift, sure speed. As always he called no attention to himself. But now the central business section of the city rose up across the dog's path. His swift steady progress had brought him to the main street of the town. The wide street was one surge and roar of traffic. Coloured lights flashed on all the buildings, innumerable lights, weird flashings. He had seen it all before from the police car, but now he wasn't seeing it from the safety of a car, now it confronted him, and now he was alone.

On the pavement of Main Street in the midst of the business section the little dog came to a baffled halt. He edged to the curb, then stood again, unsure, bewildered. Cars rushed in front of him, crowds of people passed behind him on the pavement. But he had to cross the busy street, for his instinct told him that beyond it lay the dogs' home, far beyond.

Main Street to him was like an awful river he would have to cross. It barred his path with its bewildering surges of traffic. It confused him with its noises, lights, and crowds. He tried to keep away from the people. He sat small and anonymous on the very edge of the curb halfway along the street. He was baffled. His instinct urged him to go, but the busy street frustrated the urge.

In his helplessness and frustration the haunted, lost feeling came over him as it had so often in the lonely back fields in the country. He could not swallow it. He whined, but the miserable little piping sound was lost in the busy city noises.

Farther down the street a man also stood alone at the edge of the curb – stood there bemused, watching the flow of traffic, the crowds, the buildings, the lighted windows. He was in a blue sea captain's uniform. He held a little pad hidden in one big hand, and from time to time he sketched quick lines on the pad and then studied the busy scene again. The thin small sounds of the dog's whining came to his ears. He listened to the out-of-place sound, then beyond a dustbin at the curb he saw the little dog.

The big man stayed where he was, but he ripped a page from his pad, crumpled it into his pocket, and rapidly began sketching again. But now he was sketching the small dog on the curb. The little dog, his eyes riveted on the street, enveloped in his own misery, was unaware of the man.

Both man and dog were so intent on what they were doing neither took notice of a small flurry that suddenly developed on the sidewalk behind the little dog. A child dropped a bag of tiny chocolates directly before the entrance to a smart clothes shop. The hurrying crowd swirled and eddied around the mess on the sidewalk.

The big man finished his sketch. Then he walked over to the little dog. 'What's the matter, fellow, are you lost? You look so out of place!' The little dog swallowed, stopped crying, and looked up at the big man. The blue uniform reassured him. He waited, held himself still.

At that moment a man with a broom emerged from the clothes shop and began briskly sweeping the spilled chocolates towards the curb. He worked fast with quick hurried swipes of the broom. A last long sweep of the broom towards the curb just touched the little dog. As if shot the dog leaped straight into the street, directly into the path of a car. The big, uniformed man lunged after him. He swept the dog up in his hands, whirled and leaped back to the curb.

A policeman, who had been directing traffic at the corner, came hurrying over. 'Everything okay, Captain?' He eyed the little dog in the big man's arms. 'Kind of foolish risking your life for that, wasn't it?'

'Oh, I don't know,' the big man said. The policeman returned to his corner, but the big man stood studying the quiet little dog in his arms. He pinched the dog's narrow stomach experimentally. 'Hm, a hollow little sepulchre. You can stand something to eat. Come on, let's go and eat, you and I. You've earned a big meal for that nice little sketch.'

Quiet and resigned the little dog let himself be carried down the street, although his instinct told him it was leading him away from the direction of the dogs' home. But the man was holding him and the little dog yielded. He had surrendered. The big man studied the different restaurants they came to, trying to find one that looked as if it might not object to a dog.

On a side street he at last found what he had been looking for — a hamburger wagon. The door stood open and the big man poked his head inside. 'Any objections to a dog if I keep him in my lap?' he asked. His big voice boomed through the bar inside.

'Anybody got any objections to a dog,' the cook in white cap and grease-spotted apron yelled from the rear of the bar to the customers.

'No, why?' a man said. 'Bring him in.'

No one objected. The captain seated himself on the first stool at the narrow counter that ran along the wall of the bar.

'What's yours?' the cook yelled.

'A hamburger and coffee for me, and a heaped plate of mince for the dog,' the captain said. He looked down at the little dog. 'You're not much, are you?' he whispered. 'But starting with the mince we'll build you into something, you just watch.'

'Come and get it,' the cook yelled out.

The captain got up. Then he stood and looked rather helpless. 'I hate to let go of the dog, and I'm afraid I haven't got hands enough,' he said apologetically to no one in particular. 'Oh, sit down,' a man at the far end of the counter yelled at him. 'We'll slide it along to you.'

They slid the food and coffee from person to person along the counter until it reached the captain at the far end. He looked at the small plate of mince. 'This little fellow is starved. I'm afraid that's hardly enough,' he said dubiously to the woman on the stool next to him.

'Hey, Al,' the woman yelled at the cook. 'The man says you're too stingy with the dog. He wants another plateful, and pile it on this time.'

'Okay, okay,' the cook yelled back.

The little dog gulped the food. The second plate came sliding from hand to hand along the counter.

On the busy street corner, the captain tried to board a bus with the rest of the people, but the bus driver saw the dog. 'Sorry, no dogs,' he said with finality. 'Company rules – no dogs.'

The captain backed down the steps again. 'Then how am I going to get home?' he asked plaintively.

'Had you thought of ditching the dog?'

'No, I hadn't, since I don't intend to.'

'Then it looks like walking,' the bus driver told him. 'What's the matter with a taxi?'

'Taxi!' the captain's face lit up. 'Do you know I never thought of that? Thank you.'

The bus driver looked curiously at his uniform. 'Yes, I suppose you are kind of lost if you can't get home by boat.'

The captain laughed. 'It's something like that,' he admitted.

The taxi he hailed screeched to a halt and the captain opened the door. 'Is it all right?' he asked. 'I'll keep my dog in my lap. That won't get hair all over your seat.'

'Sure, anything,' the taxi driver said carelessly. He looked at the little thin dog. 'Where did you pick him up?' he asked. 'Where to – dogs' home?'

'Oh, no,' the captain said hastily. 'I'm adopting him, but I live out in the country. I don't know if you'll go that far.'

'Mister, I'll take you to heaven if you're willing to pay for it.'

'Then we're all set,' the captain said, relieved. He relaxed and settled his bulk in the seat. 'Now we're all right,' he said gratefully. 'I don't like town,' he informed the taxi driver. 'Carlisle Road. It's five miles west of town.'

The driver nodded. They set off at furious pace. The big man in the middle of the back seat nervously steadied himself with a long arm thrust against the edge of each window. The little dog stood tense and alert on his lap. 'I'm in no hurry,' the captain said at last. 'In fact, I can pay you a little more if that helps *you* not to be in a hurry.'

The driver grinned. 'Look,' he pointed, 'there's the dogs' home now. That little grey building back there.'

The captain obediently looked but said nothing. The taxi tore on. The driver at times ventured abrupt opinions on things, but got little response from the back seat. The big man brooded over the little dog, who had gone to sleep in his lap.

'What do you see in him?' the driver said at last. He got no answer.

The tight city and the mathematical streets were gone. The town sprawled out into the country. The man rolled down the windows on both sides, breathed deep, inhaled the country air with his whole body. 'Next to big stretches of water, big stretches of land are the best,' he observed. 'Space.'

The driver did not hear him. He had opened the

throttle, and the ancient cab rattled and bowled along the highway at jolting speed. The dog suddenly woke up, not from the roar of the car, but from the feel and smell of the country. In one jump he was at the window. He thrust his nose out, his whole head. He sniffed the familiar smells. The man watched him. 'Are you home now, too?' he asked the little dog.

The dog's tail waved against the man's chest, but all of his head was outside the cab; the wind sang along his ears.

'I wish you'd slow down,' the big man told the driver, for the first time impatient.

'You're the boss,' the driver said. He shrugged. 'The old bus will still go, won't it?'

The man and the dog stared at the fields going by. In a deep meadow were seven cows and two peaceful horses. 'Now we'll soon be home,' the man told the dog. 'It's the big white house among the pines, coming up now,' he told the driver. He was leaning forward.

'Quite a house,' the driver observed. 'You must have quite a family.'

'No, I live alone,' the captain said. 'I need space.'

'Well, now you'll at least have a dog – such as he is.'

'He's one that needs space, too,' the captain said.

15. THE HEAVENLY WEEK

The week in the big quiet house with the big quiet man was heaven, pure heaven. The big man was gentle and quiet and kind. And like the old man at the dogs' home he gave food, much food, regular food. But unlike the old man at the dogs' home he also gave the little dog freedom – the freedom of a whole enormous twelve-room house with stairs and attic and basement. Rooms and rooms to flit through, stairs to rush up, stairs to plunge down. Rough carpets to slide the whole body over in sensuous rub-down delight. He could come and go in security, in safety, and in ownership. The wonderfulness lay in that – the feeling of ownership. For the first time in all his insecure life! It was a new experience, a new sense – the growing sense of ownership.

After a whole serene week the house was beginning to be his house. All his! He was free to come, free to go, chase upstairs, plunge down to the basement, search the attic, peer out of high upstairs windows at the wide stretches of countryside. The little dog did not have the slightest hankering for the outdoors of the countryside. He'd had that too long; now he had a house. It was heaven.

He had a house and a big quiet man who talked to him in quiet understanding. Under the big booming voice there was nothing but kindness. Already the little dog sensed that the voice had to boom, but in the boom there were no orders for him, no reprimands, no punishings. It gradually began to form in the little dog's mind that this man accepted him as he was, that he didn't have to be something different, do differently from what he was doing, do something better. At the end of the week he did not hesitate any more before rushing up the carpeted stairway and rushing right down again. He did not feel vaguely guilty any more after he had done such things. He no longer was confused and unsure as to whether he had done right or wrong – the way he had always felt in that faraway grim house of his puppy days.

He did not do things wholeheartedly yet. He was still too grave and earnest and quiet about everything he did. He did not know how to show his emotions even when he felt his best and happiest, throwing himself up the carpeted stairs and pummelling right down again. It was play, but he had to learn to play, so while learning he had to be serious and intent about his play. But once when he'd stood for a long time looking out of a high window, both front feet planted on the window sill, he had almost begun to feel a little bold. It was a fine, new feeling.

He had not entirely accepted the captain yet. Oh, he might gradually come to it, but not in one week. As yet he just surrendered, just yielded.

He would sit in the man's lap when the man picked him up. They'd sit for hours staring out of a window at the evening twilight and the change of moods that came in the still countryside. But he never jumped up of his own accord, he never jumped down. He did not even follow the man around the house. He went about the house alone.

And still – sometimes when he was all alone in a room lying in luxury on a deep carpet, he would hear the captain humming to himself while working on a painting in a faraway closed room. Suddenly joy would flood his little dog soul. Then the sweet urge would come to go to the man, and he would wag his tail. But the moment he would hear his tail slap the carpet, he would stop it. He still needed to be quiet and silent and unnoticed – the silence of the fugitive. He would stop his tail, but his eyes would be big and bright and moist. With his face stretched on his paws he would lie watchful, waiting for another sound from the man he was beginning to love.

He was learning to love, he was trying to learn, but there was so much inside of him still in the way. The one thing not in his way was the big man himself. He was patient, he made no demands, he did not try to hurry the little dog along. He understood.

On the next to last day of that first good week, the little dog was at an upstairs window, feet planted tensely on the window sill. The whole house was silent; the big man had gone out. The little dog had trotted through every room of the house, deliberately, seriously. He was not searching for the man – he knew the man was out – but he was experiencing a new feeling – the grave, deep feeling of responsibility. The house had been left to him. Now that he had gone through the whole house, he stood at the window, re-connoitring, on guard.

At that responsible moment a huge, dark dog came loping down the road on an important errand of his own. The dog just jogged along, looking straight ahead, but fury suddenly raged in the little dog's throat. Not because of the big dog, but because of the big house that was his! Safe behind the high window his fury rattled itself out in high, swift, coughing barks. It was for the house, a warning. 'It's mine, be gone, stay away, this house is mine!'

The big dog on the road paid little or no attention, loped carelessly along. In the house the little dog followed the dog on the road from window to window as long as he could keep him in sight. Driving him on, trying to drive him away with the rattling fury of his barking. When the big dog at last was gone the little dog retreated to the centre of the room. Suddenly he stood stock-still, awed by himself. He stood pert, head cocked, still feeling the hotness of his throat from the fury of his barking. The dog was gone, the house was safe and still. Once more, prancing more firmly now, stiff-legged, head up, he made the rounds of all the rooms. He even went to the attic.

Back in the first room, he went to the window for

a last reconnoitring look at the road. Immediately he stiffened. There was the dark dog again, but there was the master too. The captain was coming back and the strange dog was trotting at his heels. A terrible fury rose. The little dog attacked the window while his barking machine-gunned out of him. He threatened the dog, he scolded his master. He was outraged that the dog had dared to come back, and he was jealous. Then the captain stopped, patted the big dog. The dog wagged a bushy tail. The little dog coughed his staccato barks; he flung himself at the window.

Now the master came up the drive; the big dog stopped in the road. At least he had halted the dog. Again bold and full of hate behind the window, the little dog raged to the attack. He was so intent on the dog planted there in the road that he was scarcely aware the captain had come upstairs and stood behind him in the room. The big dog loped off. The little dog turned to race to another window. There stood the man! In one moment the flush of victory, the triumph, the confidence oozed out of him. He cringed to the carpet, tried to drag himself on rubbery legs across the carpet to the man. His tail dragged miserably.

'No! No!' the captain said. 'Don't do that now. You were right – you did right. It's your house. You're a good dog. You are a very good dog.'

He did not know what to do – he was being praised! He wanted to believe it, accept it, but his legs were rubber, and his tail trembled against his undersides, so tightly did it want to paste there. He had done right, he had done nothing wrong – all that was in the man's praising voice, but he could not believe it. His scared body wouldn't let him believe it.

The man hunched down beside him and stroked him. 'Good dog, good dog. You are a very good dog.' And while the little dog still could not believe it, he filed it away to remember, and he even managed to get to his feet. But later, after the master had gone to his room, the little dog patrolled the house again, except the attic. He did it gravely, thoroughly. And his tail was not between his legs.

That day marked a great change in the dog – his first feeling of ownership and possession and responsibility for the house. And that feeling, could he have held it, would have taken him a long way to feeling possessive about the man. But the next day was cleaning day.

The captain explained it to the little dog. He stood before a closed closet, talking deliberately. 'Today is going to be different from what you've become used to in this week. Once a week I clean this house and make it shipshape – just shipshape, not a woman's fussy way of cleaning, but you've got to keep things under control.'

He made a point of talking deliberately to the dog, for he had noted that for the first time the little dog had come of himself to stand beside him. It had started this morning. From time to time the dog had left his silent rounds of the house to come and stand beside him. It would be for only a moment, then he would trot off on his own little private missions again, but the man had sensed that the little dog was beginning to accept him.

Now the dog stood, head cocked, inquisitively eyeing the door, tense to know what lay behind this door, one of the few that had not yet been opened to him.

'You'll be disappointed,' the captain told him. 'It's just a broom closet, nothing for you to guard.' As he talked he pulled the door open. Something knocked and rattled against the opening door, and then two dust mops and a broom clattered to the floor. The man stooped, picked up the broom. 'I sure didn't have that closet shipshape, did I?' He turned. The little dog was gone. The man looked around, completely surprised. 'Now how'd he do that so fast and so quietly? He vanished like a ghost,' he said to himself. 'Queer, when he was so curious about what was behind the door.'

He suddenly straightened, listened. There came a panicky scrabbling against the back door. The man, broom in hand, walked to the back of the house. The little dog, desperately scratching at the door, turned, saw the man and the broom. Now he was cornered before the door. Cornered by the broom.

'No, I can't allow that yet,' the captain said. 'Your going out. You've first got to feel this house is yours so you'll automatically come back to it.' He stepped up, broom still in his hand, to shove the door more securely on its latch.

There came the broom! The little dog backed against the door, faced it. His hackles rose, his lips pulled back from his teeth. He growled a warning, but a pitiful little whine sneaked in among his dangerous growls. This man, this big kind man came with a broom, too. Always they came with brooms. But then he became confused for the broom didn't come prodding and poking and hurting. The man stood leaning on the broom, looking sorrowfully down at him. 'Now what? Now what, little fellow?' he said over and over. 'Two moments ago you were normal.'

He pulled the broom back between his feet. At that moment the little dog catapulted out of his corner, whipped past the man's legs and out of the kitchen. He raced through rooms, up the stairs, and to the narrow stairway that led to the attic. He crawled away into a far dusty corner under the eaves. He lay flat, scared, listening.

He heard them all – all the heavy sounds of the man through all the rooms, and always they came closer, closer. Now the big man was upstairs. The man was talking all the time in his slow, kind voice. The man was talking to him as if he were there. Not calling, not ordering, not threatening – just talking. Now the stairway to the attic creaked under his weight. He was coming. Pressed under the low roof, the dog squirmed himself back even farther. There came the man rising up into the attic, his head, his shoulders. There came the broom. He had the broom! He was coming with the broom!

Although he was hiding, the little dog had to growl and snarl to warn the broom away while it still was at a distance, while he still had some courage before the broom came close. On came the man, stooping his great height under the roof. At a little distance from the cowering dog he hunched down; he laid the broom down on the attic floor. 'Now why do you do this? Why do you hide way up here, and of what are you so desperately afraid that you have to snarl and growl and threaten me?'

Suddenly the man grabbed the broom, shoved it over the floor towards the dog. The little dog rose up to meet it, even though he was squeezed against the rafter. His ears lay back, his lips pulled back from his teeth. Hateful and ugly and fierce he charged out of his corner at the broom, but suddenly his legs went rubbery, and a puppyish whine came retching out of his throat. He backed away and tried to bury himself in the narrow space under the roof.

'So that's it. So it's the broom. I had to make sure. So they used to punish you with a broom!' The man rose up; he marched away across the attic with the broom. He jerked the attic window open. 'Now look,' he ordered. 'Now watch this well. There it goes. See it?' He hurled the broom out of the window; he turned and spread his empty hands for the little cowed dog in the far end of the attic to see. And then he hunched down at the attic window and waited for the little dog.

There were long moments of total silence in the attic, but then at last the little dog pulled himself out of hiding. And then he came in spurts across the attic. His tail still seemed to want to cling between his legs, but all of him, all but his tail, understood. Humbly grateful, and a little ashamed, he rubbed against the man and let himself be taken into the man's lap. He sat there looking meekly at the great man – the great, good, understanding man. He sat worshipping! The man sat looking down at him, and they two were quiet.

Unobtrusively, little by little, the dog loosened his tail from its cleaving to his undersides – little by little because he was ashamed now. He wanted to lick the big face brooding above him, but he was ashamed. He wanted to wag his tail, wave it, the urge was there, but he was ashamed. So he just worshipped.

The captain slowly pivoted on his heels and turned the little dog to the window to let him see the broom. There hung the broom. It had been flung into a pine tree. There it hung foolishly between the earth and sky. 'There it is,' the captain said, 'and there it stays. No more brooms in this house. We'll use the vacuum cleaner and the carpet sweeper; the house came with those, too. No more brooms. It's much better to have some dirt in the house than the dirt of fear in your heart. Later you and I will lick the brooms.'

The little dog listened gravely, and looked at the helpless broom.

'So when you were little and defenceless they came at you with brooms, did they? I know how it feels, and you needn't be ashamed. A broom or a constant kicking around when you are little, it's hard to overcome. I've had sixty years to overcome it, and you but a year or so, so don't be ashamed of yourself, little fellow. It's bad enough that I still am at times. . . . But you ought to have a name. I didn't even know how to call you when I was searching for you. And a name gives you something – a personality, I guess. But what is your name?'

The man talked softly, and the broom hung in the pine tree. A soft, sweet restfulness seeped into the little dog's soul. Now he was home, he had a house, he loved a man. He trembled. It got too much for him. He had to jump from the lap and tear in mad circles around the attic so that the dust rose. Bigger and bigger widening circles until they brought him right back to the great, good man.

The captain closed the window, and with the little dog behind him went down the attic stairs. At the bottom of the stairs the captain turned. 'I guess now you belong to me, and I and the house belong to you. That's what it means, doesn't it?'

And gravely the little dog looked down at him from the middle step of the attic stairs. And gravely he waved his thin little tail.

16. THE HIKE

The captain and the little dog stood just inside the back door of the house. The captain, his hand on the doorknob, turned to the little dog. 'Let's see, it's a whole week you've been with me now. You've made the house yours, and you know now that you belong to me. So now this is going to be our first long hike in the country together, but since I belong to you, you promise to stay with me, don't you?'

The tip of the dog's tail waved vaguely.

'There are going to be many of these hikes in our life to come, but this first one is going to be at night. Why at night? Let me explain it to you – there are brooms in my life, too. I think that's the real explanation. But if you asked me, I wouldn't honestly tell you that. I would say it had to be at night because there's a certain scene – a bridge over a creek – that I want to paint by moonlight. Yes, that's what I would say.'

The man stood brooding for a while.

'You see, all my life I wanted to paint, but all my life I had to be on boats, from the time I was kicked around as a cook's helper. And I *was* kicked. Now it's too late, and I'm ashamed, so I paint at night. Oh, I sketch by day, because I can hide a sketch pad in my big hand, but I can't hide an easel, and when people see an easel they come to stand and stare. And then I want to snarl and bite, the way you do at brooms. But instead I become self-conscious and ashamed – a great big six-footer sitting there on a little stool with a little camel's-hair brush between his knotty fingers. Then I pack up my paints and my easel and silently sneak away with my tail between my legs – the way you do with brooms.'

The man chuckled a little. 'Well, I thought I had to explain it to myself by explaining it to you. Do you see now why I picked you up? You and me, two of a kind. But tonight is the last night. After tonight we'll paint in broad daylight, we'll paint in a crowd – if I want to paint, me a big broad six-footer, why shouldn't I paint? Who's to stop me but the brooms that have been rammed into my thin hide?'

The little dog sat listening so gravely the captain suddenly boomed a big laugh. The dog waggled his tail, swept the floor with it as he kept sitting looking up at the man. 'No, you won't run away,' the big man said. 'Even if you've been a stray all your life, you won't run away.'

He opened the door. The moonlight was so bright in the yard it seemed to fall into the house with the opening of the door. The startled little dog jumped back. The captain laughed. 'It can startle you, moonlight, can't it – soft as it is?'

Out in the yard, the dog, a bit ashamed of his scare, raced out before the man, then came back to him in queer gyrations and circles. He made mad little hopping dashes at shadows, performed, showed off. But in the end he came back to the man to look up at his face for approval, stood looking a little foolish.

The captain laughed and shook his head. 'It's no use, I've found. It just makes you feel foolish. If you didn't learn to play when you were young, you never quite get used to it. Maybe they made us old too soon . . . But go ahead, I promise I won't laugh at you, because I feel so good myself . . . Let's race!'

The man tucked the folded easel high under his arm and started off at a hard run. The little dog kept

pace beside him. Then to show the man, he suddenly spurted ahead, shot away into a copse, and came back in a wide, unnecessary, hard-racing circle. They both stood panting.

'Now you're showing off,' the captain panted. 'I know you can run better than I can, but you can't paint as well as I can.' He boomed such a big laugh over his own joke, it resounded out of the shadowy copse. He listened to it. 'Hey!' he said, surprised. 'Listen to that laugh, will you? Maybe you and I can learn to play yet. Maybe between us two.'

They marched on again. 'It's a stiff hike,' the man told the dog. 'It's still a few miles. I ought to know. I hate to tell you how often I've marched out to that bridge – just to study it, before I got up the nerve to try and paint it. By night, of course . . . Jackass! Not you – me,' he explained.

The little dog was not listening. He had become tense, alert. They were coming into country that he knew; they were on the edge of his old territory. Every fence, every hedgerow, every dog path was familiar in the shadowy moonlight. He was back. These were his haunts. Here he had lived, here he had starved and sung out his loneliness and lovelessness. But now he wasn't alone. Now the big man had him, and he had the great, good man. Instinctively he drew close, stayed right at the captain's heels, as if the man might suddenly disappear, and he would be alone again in the old loneliness of his old hopeless life.

By moonlight they crossed the well-known territory, the man walking sturdily, the little dog tight at his heels. Along a distant road the houses rose stark in the moonlight – the houses where he had scrounged for crumbs and table leavings and food left over by chickens. From one of the houses a dog on guard bayed at their distant noises, warned them off. 'You keep your distance. You stay away from this place.'

As in the old days other dogs took up the warning. The telegraphy of dog barks ran down the road from house to house until it faded away in a far distance. The countryside had been put on the alert by the two night intruders – the heavy tread of the man, the faint scent of the little dog. They told each other, the watchdogs: 'Watch it. They've been along here; they're heading your way. Watch it.'

The man twisted his head and looked down at the little dog crowding his heels. 'Sticking close, aren't you. Is it because of the dogs? Don't look so worried; you needn't be ashamed that you're afraid of those other dogs. After all, you're small and you're in their territory, and they on their own grounds. But that's what I'm for – to protect you on strange ground. When we're at home you're to guard me and the house and warn off strangers. Remember, that's the arrangement between us from now on.'

The little dog waved his tail and looked up at the man. He loved being talked to like this. It was especially marvellous here, going through the old lonely territory – being talked to!

Now they were crossing the back of the farm where Butch, the toothless old hound, had lived. There rose the house. In spite of the distant barking of dogs, he couldn't resist but quickly left the man and crossed to the yard. Beside the shed he pawed for a moment at the sack under which old Butch had buried his bones. He wasn't hungry, he didn't need food; it was just an old habit and an old memory. He tore back to the man.

Later the captain crossed flat fields to the creek that the dog knew so well. They followed the creek's winding through the field. Moonlight glistened in the gurgling water. 'What a night!' the man exclaimed.

But the dog once more had to leave the man. This time to race across flat fields to the old pile of kindling at the edge of the pine copse. He briefly dodged under the sagging woodpile, through the same small tunnel opening where he had whined out his first puppy nights in the big fearsome unknown country.

As he backed from under the pile to search out the man again there was a dark thin shadow under the pines. With wolfish stealth a big dog lunged from the shadows and pounced. The surprised little dog uttered one cut-off yelp. The police dog was so huge, there was no defence. The little dog let himself be carried along with the lunge of the bigger dog, let himself roll to get clear. Then he jumped to his feet and ran. From old habit he twisted and dodged as he ran out before the big dog, got a row of shrubs between him and the attacker. Old habit sent him circling back to the safety of the woodpile. The big dog came on, was gaining, ran alongside of him now, either to head him off or to grab his front leg. Suddenly the little dog threw himself back in an agile, weasel-like turn. It was an old manoeuvre to gain time. But it had turned him, and now he was running away from the woodpile. Like lightning it suddenly flashed through his brain – he did not need the safety of the woodpile; he had the man!

He fled, raced silently just ahead of the gaining police dog. As he neared the captain the little dog let out one long yelp for warning and for help. The captain whirled, saw the two dogs racing down on him. 'Hey, you!' he said. That was all that was needed. The next moment the huge silent dog was a shadowy streak over the moonlit fields. The little dog stared after him.

'You don't know how glad I am you came to me,' the captain said. Without looking back at the police dog, the captain walked on again. It was that simple, that easy, that safe! The little dog walked close beside the man, marvelling.

Together they followed the creek. At times the dog sprinted out ahead of the man, short, hard little runs – very short, so that he could turn and tear back, because it felt so good to run back to the man.

'Ah, it's going to be fine,' the captain told him each time. The dog kept up his private little game until the creek began to cut deep under wooded hills. They walked along the creek bed, close along the high, sheer bank that the creek had dug itself along the bottom of the hills. The bank was higher than the big man's shoulders.

The little dog walked out ahead now, gravely and sedately. He listened for the man's footsteps coming behind him, pacing himself to keep just a few steps ahead of them. He was leading the way. Now the creek curled around the hill. Suddenly the little dog stopped. Ahead loomed the bridge. There was the high bridge over the creek. The same bridge where the girl, Catherine, had lost him as a puppy. But if the dog remembered he gave no sign, he was too intent about something on the tree-darkened hill. He stood tense, listening.

The man came on, but the little dog blocked his path. Something had made him uneasy. A tiny growl forced itself out of his throat, but he cut it off. The man stopped. He, too, stood listening. 'It's all right,' he whispered at last. 'There's nothing.' For some reason he had lowered his voice. The little dog did not relax. Now he stared hard at the bridge.

'I know it's dark and gloomy under the bridge,' the captain said reassuringly, 'but we'll just cross under and climb up to the road on the other side. It's too steep on this side.' His voice was hushed.

The little dog stood listening, but not to the words. He was listening to things farther up the hill under the dark gloom of the trees that shut out the moonlight. He sensed rather than heard. It was more an awareness, a feeling that he and the man were not alone. Again he looked up at his master, and kept blocking his path. But the captain stepped over him. 'It's nothing.' Then the little dog could do nothing but follow.

It was black under the bridge, and as they stepped under it something plopped into the water. It startled both the man and dog. The dog stood still, then he shot forward, all his misgivings concentrated on the splash in the water. The captain, too, stole to the water's edge. 'What was it?' he whispered. 'A frog? A muskrat maybe. Is that what you've been hearing?' The water rustled under the bridge. 'Couldn't you get him?'

The dog stood still, intent on whatever it was that had jumped into the stream. The captain used the time to put down his easel and fill his pipe. 'Secret under here, isn't it?' he said softly. But the dog suddenly lost interest in the water, and stood with one paw uplifted, head cocked towards the high planking of the bridge above them. A tiny growl started out of him, became a questioning whimper. 'Now what?' the captain said, and picked up the easel and walked from under the bridge.

The captain started climbing up the same water-cut gully that the girl, Catherine, had clawed up in that storm-swept day a year or more ago. The little dog clambered up behind the captain. This time there was no broom in his path, no soggy slime and wetness, but he was restless and uneasy, and suddenly he stopped.

The man climbed on. Now his head and shoulders rose up out of the gully, rose up beside a car parked at the very edge of the road. He gasped and stopped. But the big man in a blue uniform rising up suddenly as if out of the ground startled whoever was in the car. A seat spring lurched. And then out of the dark, silent car fire belched.

The little dog staring up from the gulley saw the fire spurt from the car. The shot so near, so close, shattered the night. The captain jumped back, lost his balance, windmilled his arms, came crashing down. The dog saw him falling, the man, his wild arms, the easel he clutched. And then the easel caved down over his back.

At that split moment there was another spurt of flame and the gun blast. The roar was in the dog's ears, but an awful smashing numbness was in his hind leg. Then the crash of the man and the easel slammed him to the ground. The dog yelped, struggled wildly, madly pushed and pulled himself from under the easel. He squirmed free. He pelted away and left the fallen man behind. Headlong he fled under the bridge, headlong down the creek. On and on in pain and terror.

Then suddenly it was again as it had been under the bridge and along the creek that other time of lightning flame and thunder crashings. As he threw himself on along the creek the whole hillside above him seemed to come alive with crashings and spurts of flame. Short, sharp single shots at first, but then among that shooting began the rat-a-tat-tat of a tommy gun. It coughed and rattled; continuous balls of fire spurted down the hillside.

Before that sound, the fire and the flame, the little dog threw himself ahead still faster. In his hurt and pain and fright he instinctively did the same thing he had done before as a puppy. Beyond the hills he left the creek and hurtled over the fields towards his old pile of kindling. He crawled under it, and hid.

Under the woodpile the little dog lay, softly whining to himself. Tenderly he licked his wounded haunch where the fire from the car had hit him, where it burned. The numbness of the hard bullet blow was leaving his haunch; the tiny bullet hole smarted and stabbed and burned. He licked at the spot again, but he became nauseated by the pain. He retched, and softly he whined in the misery of his pain and bewilderment and lostness.

He did not know about guns and bullets; he did not know he had been shot. The piercing pain and slamming numbness had come when the big man had crashed down on him, when the man had slammed the easel down on him. In one moment at the old bridge, the great good man had undone all the goodness of the great good week. Under the woodpile the little dog lay sorrowing.

17. CANDY OR JINX

The next morning the front page of the town's morning paper was full of the two stories. The screaming headlines told the story of the daring daylight bank robbery, and, fitting right in with it, the story of Captain Carlson in his sea captain's uniform, accompanied by a little dog, blundering into the bank robbers' car at the tense moment when practically the town's whole police force, the sheriff and his deputies and hastily armed posses were closing in on it.

Big black headlines, news stories and pictures covered the whole front page. There were pictures of the bridge and the riddled car. There were separate rogues' gallery pictures of the two dead bank robbers, pictures taken when they had been in prison. There was a picture of Captain Carlson in his seaman's uniform. There was even a picture of the little stray dog, but this was not a photograph – the newspaper had reproduced the sketch that the captain had made of him sitting small and hopeless on Main Street in the middle of the downtown section. The newspaper pointed out – just for reader interest – that the sketch had been made with the little dog sitting directly opposite the

First National Bank, the bank that had been robbed.

There was a special story devoted to the little dog. CANDY or JINX the black headline asked. There was a picture of one of the police officers who had taken Candy to the hospital. The police officer told how Candy had first been found by the pig woman. The pig woman – that is what the newspaper called her; they said that she had insisted on being called that – had immediately met with an accident upon adopting the little dog, but just before the accident the woman had found out that the stray's name was Candy. And now Captain Carlson, who had adopted him only a week or so ago, had also met with an accident, and the bank, opposite which the dog had been sitting when sketched, had been robbed. Two accidents and a bank robbery. CANDY or JINX?

The story ended, however, that in spite of any such jinx, Captain Carlson, the retired sea captain, was offering a fifty-dollar reward for the stray dog. And it told how the captain, in spite of a broken leg, had refused to stay at the hospital to which he had been taken, but had returned home the same night in the hope that if the little dog hadn't been too badly wounded he might return to the captain's home.

The girl Catherine and her brother George, leaving the house to go to school, found their newspaper lying on the porch. The girl glanced at the rolled newspaper. It was as if the sketch of the little dog leaped up at her. 'Why, that's Candy!' she said, startled. 'George, look, that's Candy!'

They burst into the house. 'Mother, Mother! Mother, where are you? Candy's picture is in the paper!'

Their mother came hurrying from the kitchen. 'What are you two screaming about? What's happened?'

133

'Candy's picture is in the paper!'

'Candy? Candy?' the woman said impatiently. 'Oh, that's right, that was the name you gave the puppy. What about him?'

'I don't know,' the girl said, 'but look, here's his picture. Somebody drew his picture.'

Her mother opened the paper and spread it out on the dining table. Together they leaned over the table, their eyes racing to take in all the news at once. The boy's eyes leaped to the picture of the bridge.

'Mom, look!' he yelped. 'There's the bridge where Catherine lost Candy. Look at that car. It's standing almost exactly where our car was when that road caved in. But it's full of bullet holes.'

The woman was reading, absorbed. 'Yes,' she said

hastily. 'Only your father and a bank robber would ever pick a road like that.'

'But what happened, Mom? What happened? And what about Candy?' the boy demanded. He tried to absorb the story from the pictures and the headlines, but it was too confusing. 'What happened?' he insisted impatiently. 'Did Candy belong to the bank robbers?'

'If you'd only let me read,' his mother said. 'I've first got to find out, haven't I?'

The boy hardly heard it. He had become absorbed in spelling out the big letters above a black-bordered box at the bottom of the front page. 'Fifty Dollars Reward for a Stray,' he read slowly.

'Hey, Mom! There's fifty dollars reward for Candy. Fifty dollars! And we got him for only a dollar and fifty cents.' No one paid any attention, but the boy tried to read no more. He stood back trying to digest the thought of the fifty-dollar reward.

'Well, what a story!' the mother said, straightening out at last. She turned to the boy. 'Well, I hardly know where to begin,' she began, 'but the First National Bank in the city centre was robbed yesterday. Two men came in just before closing time, and, imagine, they got nineteen thousand dollars! The paper says it's the biggest bank robbery in our town's history. Anyway, they made a very quick getaway. But the police were on their trail almost from the start, and the police warned the whole state, and road blocks were set up everywhere on every highway to trap the bandits. But do you know what those bank robbers did? They suspected that road blocks would be thrown up, so instead of trying to crash through one of them and maybe getting shot or stopped, they doubled right back to town before they came near any road block. You see, I guess that way the police wouldn't really know whether they'd already got through before the road blocks were set up.'

'Oh, that was smart,' George said.

'Well, maybe . . . Anyway, instead of going back into town they headed .for that road where we lost Candy. And if you ask me, they couldn't have picked a better spot! You see, they'd figured if they waited until night some of the road blocks might be down, because the police would think they'd already gone beyond the road blocks, and out of the state. At least, that's what the paper thinks, but they're just guessing, too. The police shot both men dead in their car at that bridge, so nobody could ask them what their plans were.'

'But what about Candy, where does he come in?' George demanded.

'Well, you see that Captain Carlson – that big man in the uniform in that picture in the paper – he'd adopted Candy only a week or so before, and he and Candy went to the bridge that night, because the captain wanted to paint the bridge . . .'

'Not the bridge, Mother!' the girl, Catherine, interrupted. 'He wanted to paint a picture of it by moonlight.'

'Well, that's what I meant,' her mother said indignantly. 'Anyway, the police found out that the robbers were parked at that bridge. So all the time that that captain and Candy were walking along the creek to that bridge, all those big hills and woods we saw from that awful road were just literally alive with policemen and deputies and all kinds of men with guns. But do you know? Not a one of them ever saw that big captain and Candy come walking along the creek – because that creek is so deep down under those woody hills. . . . And there was that car with the robbers in it, and there up from under the bridge came Captain Carlson, by that same gully that Catherine had to crawl up. Well, you can imagine, there came that man in his uniform rising right up beside the car and the bank robbers took him for a policeman, and just like that they started shooting at him. The captain jumped back and lost his balance, and that's what saved his life. But they think that somehow a bullet hit Candy. Anyway, he's disappeared again.'

The boy looked thoughtful. 'Is that why there is a reward for Candy?'

'Yes, imagine, that man is offering fifty dollars, just for information about that silly little thing. You don't even have to find him. You see, he thinks Candy was shot, or was so scared by the gunshots that he isn't going to come near anybody for a long time. So he just wants to know where he is, so he can go and get him, because if Candy's been shot he wants to have him treated immediately.'

'He sure must think a lot of our Candy,' Catherine said.

The boy's mouth hung open as he tried to digest the whole story. He looked from his mother to his sister. 'But, Mom,' he exploded, 'if that man will give fifty dollars, we know Candy, and if we found him . . .' He turned to his sister. 'Boy, Catherine, then we could get our bikes we've been saving for. We wouldn't have to wait for my next birthday.'

'Just because you knew Candy, and had him over a year ago, doesn't help you to know his whereabouts now,' his mother pointed out.

'No, but it's the same bridge and the same creek,' the boy argued.

'And then what?' his mother demanded. 'That's where he disappeared once before.'

'Well, couldn't Catherine and me go out there to look? He maybe still knows us.'

'Yes, and then what?' the mother asked again. 'He's

been gone for a whole year; he's really not ours any more. And you know what we decided after he disappeared – no dog ever again. We promised you then that instead we'd help to get each one of you a bike on your next birthday – if you saved your money.'

'But, Mother,' George pointed out excitedly. 'That's just why! Fifty dollars just for bringing Candy to that man! Why, then we could get our bikes right away!'

He looked impatiently to his sister for support. In his young mind the puppy of over a year ago had become but a dim memory. He did not consider the dog at all. He had been excited too long about the future bike, and to wait until his next birthday seemed to be to wait for eternity.

His sister considered. 'Mother, maybe he would come to us! Wouldn't it be nice if I found him again after losing him the first time? . . . Oh, we'd take him to the man right away,' she hastily assured her mother.

Their mother looked doubtful. 'I don't know.'

'Everybody's got a bike but us,' George argued.

'Well, ask your father when he comes home. I certainly wouldn't want you two running around there alone. That awful country!'

'It's Friday,' Catherine said thoughtfully. 'If Dad could take us to Grandpa and Grandma's when he comes home tonight . . .'

'Yup,' the boy shouted. He jumped up and down. 'We'd have two whole days – Saturday and Sunday – and maybe he still knows us, maybe he'd come for us and not for anybody else, and then we'd take him to the man . . . Grandpa would go with us,' he assured his mother.

'Counting chickens!' His mother smiled at his excitement. 'Well, ask your father, see what he says when he comes home . . . And now you'd better run all the way to school, or you'll be late.'

The boy pounced on the paper. 'May I take it to show teacher and the kids that it was our dog that was shot by bank robbers? . . . Oh, boy,' he said to his sister. 'I sure hope Dad lets us go when he comes home, don't you?'

18. THE WOUND

The little dog had been under the mouldering pile of kindling a whole night and a day. He still lay in almost the same position as when he had crawled under the woodpile. He lay with his head on his forepaws, hurt eyes staring blankly ahead at nothing. He hardly stirred. The slightest motion sent jarring pain through his whole body. His eyes were bright and feverish. He burned with thirst, but the sickening pain in his cramped body kept him motionless. His hot thirst mounted and mounted, and dimly, far away, he heard the rustle of the creek.

It was sheer torture, listening to the running water. It might have dragged him from under the pile of kindling in spite of pain, but the countryside wasn't quiet. This wasn't the silent, lonely back country as he had known it in the old days. Everywhere there were stirrings. He was far away from the bridge but to his ears came the noise of the cars of the sightseers and excitement seekers who had come out from the town to view the spot where the bank robbers had been shot down. There wasn't much to see, and after viewing the bridge and the creek and the gully, many of the sightseers secretly branched out from the road to hunt for the dog pictured in the newspaper for the sake of the fifty-dollar reward.

As the day wore on some of the searching parties came close. The hidden dog heard them crashing about, heard them calling him. From all over the fields and the wooded hills they were calling his name — strange, unknown voices – calling: 'Candy, Candy, Candy.' He did not even lift his head. The little dog's fright and pain were making him hide from all people. He lay alone and sorrowed. He wanted no one.

The second night the thirst got too much for him. Almost angrily, angry at the fiercely stabbing wound, he dragged himself from under the woodpile. He bit at the wound, then for a long time he licked it, gently licking the circulation back, soothing the rawness with a soft tongue. At last he stood up. Shivering with the hurt he drew the wounded leg high under his body so that nothing could touch it. On three legs he started slowly for the creek and the sound of running water in the night.

At the shadowy creek he drank his fill, and then he drank it again. He started to hobble back to the woodpile, but he turned back to the creek and drank a third time. It revived him; it brightened his eyes and cooled his hot throat and tongue. He took a few last licks at the water then stood by the creek sensing the surroundings, sensing them with his whole alert body, feeling them out, determining where there was a movement or a rustling, and whether it was meaningless or threatened danger. It was like the old days – everything was back as it always had been.

A slight rustling, thinner, quicker than the silky rustlings of the creek meant a mouse. He turned and started stalking. Halfway up the creek bank, sheltered by tree roots, a mouse was nibbling. But pain leaped up in his stiff leg and reminded the little dog that he couldn't stalk or pounce. He stood in the night silence, frustrated, undecided. He was hungry.

Far away down a road came a long complaining howl, a watchdog with nothing to do singing out boredom, making some sound against the quiet of the night. The faraway dog howled again. The little dog

listened, and then he started out. The old habits of the past year were reasserting themselves with the old gnawing hunger. But he wasn't swift and shadowy now; he was painfully slow and careful. Even the thin touch of a weed against the paw of his drawn-up leg sent screaming pains through his bones and nerves. At times he shivered with pain. Still he made progress. He held the leg rigid under his body to numb it into deadness. From old habit, but on three legs, he headed first for the yard of Butch, the toothless old hound.

The smells around Butch's yard were old, but automatically the little dog hobbled to the old sack and tilted it up with his nose. The smells under the sack were old and stale and empty. There was nothing. He hobbled to the back door. There was nothing at the back door. Even the water pan was dry and empty. The little dog sniffed at it. There was nothing.

He turned as if to go on to the next house. He passed the sack against the shed and went on beyond to old Butch's grave. Suddenly he sat down. He was spent; the bullet wound and the long fast had badly weakened him. He swayed unsteadily. There could be no further rounds of distant houses for possible crumbs and scraps. There was only one thing left to do — somehow make his way to the other pile of kindling, the nearer pile, in the maple copse behind old Butch's farm.

It was all back. The starving, lonely life was back. He sat empty and forlorn; his head hung wearily. Suddenly he lifted his hopeless head and out of his throat sang the old misery. It went on and on without breath and without let-up. It wouldn't stop. A light flashed on in an upper window of the old house. The little dog snapped his jaws shut, shut off the miserable whining. Silently he hobbled away into the shadows, back to the pile of kindling in the maple copse.

In the house the old woman upstairs in the bed shook her husband. She was sitting bolt upright, anxiously peering at the window. The man sat up. 'What is it?' he said thickly.

'It's back,' she whispered. 'It's come back again, that whining we heard the night after we buried old Butch. It was the same whining and it came from that same spot where we buried old Butch. I heard it just as clearly.'

'Well, at least turn off the light, so I can see what's in the yard.'

The old man got stiffly out of bed, and went to the window. 'The moon's got the yard pretty well lit up, but I don't see a thing.'

'It stopped the moment I turned on the light. George, what can it be?'

The old man shrugged. 'Almost anything,' he said. 'Now don't go getting superstitious about it just because it woke you out of a bad dream maybe.'

'No, but isn't it strange – we never heard it until after Butch died. Now it's come again. It's so strange and haunted.'

'Oh, it's just some small dog moon-howling in the night. Maybe he used to come and visit Butch at night. How do we know what goes on there at night?'

The man climbed back in bed, arranged the covers to suit him, closed his eyes. The old woman lay staring up at the dim ceiling. 'Just the same,' she said softly, 'I'm not superstitious, but tomorrow I'm setting out a pan of food for him again, just like I did before. Nothing happened then, except that the little dog disappeared, but I want to see what happens now, and I'm sure I'm not superstitious.' She noticed her husband was sleeping. With a little shiver she curled herself deeper under the covers. 'I still want to see,' she told herself under her breath, 'if something that can howl out there can leave tracks.' She stared at the window, wide-eyed, answerless.

'Grandpa! Grandpa!'

The two children Catherine and George came bursting into the house. 'Are you up yet? We're way early, but we've come to find Candy. We're going to look all day and maybe even all day Sunday. We even brought our lunch.' They stood almost breathless at the table, big eyes on their grandmother, trying to tell her too many things at once. 'Dad brought us, but he's got to go right back again; he's way behind with his work and he isn't going to pick us up until to-night, so we've got all day to look for Candy, and we've even brought our lunch.'

'Candy?' the old woman said. 'What *is* all this?' She looked in bewildered amusement from the children to her husband. 'Can you fit it together?'

'Oh, don't you remember?' the boy said impatiently. 'Candy was our puppy that Catherine lost.'

'Oh,' the old lady said, 'light begins to glimmer. No, I didn't remember. That was a year ago, and I only saw the puppy once, you know.' She grinned fondly at them, fond of their dithering excitement.

Now their father came into the room. He threw a newspaper on the table. 'I see they've already got both of you up a tree. Well, they've been babbling to me about it all the way here, but hanged if I can get it all clear, so I brought the newspaper – tells all about it.' The old man was pushing a chair towards him. 'No, Dad, I can't stay, I've got to get right back to work, but there was nothing for it. I had to take them here to you first.' He turned to the children. 'And see that you have that fifty dollars for me tonight when I pick you up,' he said with mock severity.

'But, John,' his mother protested, 'at least tell us what this is all about.'

'Well, Mother, it's hopeless for me to explain. The best thing is just to let them charge off after that dog, before they both burst a blood vessel. You can read the newspaper I brought. It's something about their dog being lost a second time by a man who's willing to shell out fifty dollars for his return, and the kids think they can maybe find him . . . Keep an eye on them though, will you, Dad?'

'Oh, that would be nice,' the old lady said. 'Imagine them getting their little dog back after a year . . .'

'Oh, they don't want the dog, they want to turn him in for the fifty dollars. It's bikes they've got on the brain now. They want bikes.'

'Oh,' the grandmother said.

'Okay,' the father told the children. 'Off with both of you – start hunting. That'll give Gramp and Grandma a chance to read the paper.'

That was all the children needed. They pounded out of the room, the door slammed behind them.

After her son had left and her husband had gone to his chores, the old woman picked up the newspaper. She carried it over to the picture window to read it in her favourite rocker. She read it studiously, carefully, and then she read parts of it again. From time to time she sat staring out of the big picture window, and always her eyes went to the small open space in the field before the blackberry patch across which a little dog had used to flit.

Now there was nothing. Once she saw the girl hurry across a hill, her brother racing behind her. From time to time she could faintly hear the children calling, 'Candy, Candy, Candy.'

Finally the woman put the newspaper down and just sat and mulled things over in her mind. At last she stood up and crossed over to the telephone on the wall. 'Captain Carlson?' she asked. 'Well, this is Mrs Cook. I live a few miles down the road from you, and about three miles from the bridge where you lost your dog . . . No, I haven't found him!' she said sharply. 'But I've just read the story about it in the newspaper, and I've been putting two and two together, and maybe – just maybe, mind you – I may have some idea as to your dog's general whereabouts.

'No, now wait a minute – don't get excited and don't get your hopes up. I've told you I'm just working things out, but there are several things that I don't know that maybe you can help me with. Maybe between the two of us . . .'

She paused. 'All right, then . . . how long ago was it that the pig woman picked him up and had that accident. About two weeks? Well, two weeks ago I last heard the dog in the night – he's got a peculiar whistling spooky howl – moon-howling, my husband calls it – have you ever heard him do that? . . .

'Once when he was lost in the city? Well,' she said excitedly, 'there aren't two small dogs that would make a sound exactly like that – it was the loneliest sound. And last night I heard it again, and it was coming from the same spot it came from two weeks ago after our dog died. It makes me almost sure in my own mind that your dog and the little dog I've seen and heard around here are one and the same. And if that's so, that narrows it down, for my grandchildren lost him a year or so ago as a puppy, and since that time he must have holed up somewhere in our general area.'

She was forced to listen for a while. 'Brooms put him in a panic, you say? No, I wouldn't know. Wait a minute! The grandchildren have told me that when he was a puppy, their mother – she's overclean – used to punish him with a broom, and he'd fight the broom, and then he'd get it with the broom until he crawled . . . Well, that would be another sign that it's the same dog . . .

'No, the children don't want him back. No, definitely no! A year is a long time for a child and a dog, and their mother has insisted on no more dogs. They're all over the farm now hunting for him, but just for the fifty dollars reward, so they can get themselves bicycles. They want bicycles now.' She laughed a little woefully. 'That's how it goes. Oh, yes, his name is definitely Candy. That's the name the children gave him. I'll tell you, I'll keep the children hunting and calling. He might just remember them enough to want to come to them. But if not, then tonight I do exactly what I did two weeks ago. Tonight I'll set out food in the same spot I used to for old Butch. Then if the food is gone in the morning, we'll know he'll come again the next night, and then we can plan how to catch him.'

The captain lay on a couch, his leg stretched straight, thick and encased. He slowly replaced the telephone on its cradle and lay staring thoughtfully. Somewhere in the house a woman bustled about. She sang a little as she worked. 'That is an idea!' the captain said aloud to the room. He raised himself on an elbow. 'Martha,' he boomed. 'Martha.'

The woman came into the doorway. 'Martha,' the captain said, 'before you leave tonight cook a plateful of mince and set it out in the yard right near the back door, and leave the back door wide open.'

'Is it for the little dog?' Martha asked.

The captain nodded. 'Yes, but do it the very last thing before you leave this evening.'

'That'll be late,' the woman said severely. 'I don't know if I'll ever get this house straightened and decent. It's had such a man's cleaning all these months – a lick and a promise.'

The captain grinned. 'Well, I'm the man, so I won't notice if it isn't absolutely up to scratch, so don't worry about it. Just don't forget to cook the mince and set it out – that's important.'

19. HURRY HOME, CANDY

In the farmhouse three miles down the road from the captain's house, the old woman was standing before the big picture window again. The children had suddenly come into sight over a hill. She saw that her husband was with them. 'Of course,' she said aloud. 'How he spoils them.' She heard the children's voices, dim, distant, but clear. First the girl's voice: 'Candy, Candy, Candy.' Then the boy, like an echo: 'Candy, Candy!'

The old man trudged at a little distance behind the children. The three seemed to be gradually manoeuvring back towards the house. Now they disappeared for a while into the maple copse. The children must be getting tired, or they'd given up hope, for as they left the copse they came straight across the field towards the house. The old man still followed the fence at the edge of the copse.

Suddenly the woman at the picture window started. She was almost sure that for a moment she'd caught a brief movement at the edge of the copse, far behind her husband. Now it was gone, swallowed up in the shadows.

The old woman waited. The children had stopped calling, were plodding stolidly on. But there, there — yes, there it was again along the fence of the field in which the children were walking. The dog must be following the children along the fence. But now her husband yelled something, and started across to the children. In the moment of the man's yell there was a brief flash, and the dog was gone.

'Oh, he spoiled it. He spoiled it,' she disappointedly told herself. 'If only he hadn't been there! The little dog was coming to the children.'

She hurried across the room to the telephone, gave the operator Captain Carlson's number . . . 'I saw him,' she told the captain without any preliminaries. 'I just saw him! One brief glimpse. He was following the children at a distance. But then he heard or saw my husband. If my husband hadn't been there, he might have followed the children. But at least now we know that he's alive and around his old haunts, but it looked as if he were hobbling on three legs.'

She listened for a few brief moments. 'No, as soon as the children get to the house I'll stuff some sandwiches in their hands and send them right out again. They've been out there since dawn, but I know the moment they hear I saw him they won't be able to rest. And this time I'll keep my husband home . . . Yes, I'll keep you informed.' She hung up and hurried back to the window.

Now the fields were quite empty of callings and movements. There were no more footsteps, no more cracklings of twigs and crunchings of old dead leaves. All morning the little dog had listened to the children's voices coming, going, now near, now far, then coming back again. Always calling. 'Candy, Candy, Candy.' In the girl's high thin voice. 'Candy, Candy.' In the boy's still higher, shriller voice.

He hadn't stirred from his painful, stiff position under the pile of kindling. But the calling of his name had kept tugging at his memory – a faint, far remembrance of young voices he had once loved.

Silently, eyes staring down the tunnel-like opening under the wood, he had followed the movements of the children as they neared the pile of wood. For a

149

flash of a moment he had seen them as they blundered along on the dry twigs on the copse floor. But they left the copse. Suddenly the boy shrilled out in a last hard call: 'Candy, Candy.' There was no urging in his voice now, just tired hopelessness. The girl did not add her call. There it remained, that last call.

Suddenly an urge rose in the little dog; he pulled himself stiffly from under the woodpile and stole to the edge of the copse. But by the time he had hobbled across the copse the children were away in the field. Silently the dog stole along the edge of the field by way of the fence. He stood staring after the children, screened from them by a bush. At that moment the old man yelled across the field and walked over to the children. The dog turned away. A twig he stepped on jumped up and hit his wounded leg. He cut off one tiny whimper and hobbled back. He crawled under the woodpile again, and lay there in pain. He still heard the going-away sound of the three in the field, but he shut himself away from it into his loneliness. He stared straight ahead, and every few moments he swallowed.

The children came into the house in silent defeat. All their fine hopes of the morning were dashed – all their hopes for the bicycles. The grandfather seemed as disappointed and thwarted as the children. The boy threw himself heavily into a chair, surly with defeat, blank-faced because he was so near to tears. 'He didn't come,' he managed to tell his grandmother.

'I guess he's forgotten us,' the girl said bitterly.

The old man said nothing.

'We ate our lunch, but we're still hungry,' George told his grandmother. He looked hungrily at the sandwiches on the table.

'I guess he's forgotten us,' the girl said again. 'We never saw anything of him.' She was too sullen with disappointment to be interested in the food.

'No, but I saw him!' their grandmother said. 'I saw him, and he started to follow you, and if it hadn't been for your grandfather yelling at you at that moment, he might have come. But the moment he saw a man he disappeared.'

'Where, Grandma? Did you really see him? Where?'

'Coming out of our copse. So now you grab some sandwiches, and you two get right back there, and this time without your grandfather. But don't hunt around that copse, don't go poking and searching for him – just play! Play some of the games you played when he was a puppy. Talk to each other and mention his name a lot, but don't go crashing around looking for him. Then if he still doesn't come, walk away from the copse every now and then as if you were starting for home. I'll be watching to see if he comes out again. Do you think you can do that?'

The children nodded solemnly, awed by all their grandmother seemed to know about the little dog. Then George grabbed a handful of sandwiches. 'Come on, Catherine, let's go!'

After the children were gone the old woman went to the telephone to make her latest report. The captain listened carefully, and then he told her: 'Now that I know where he is, and that he's alive – you understand the children are going to get bicycles for all they've done. And it certainly sounds to me that you've figured it out the best way – having the children play around him as in the old days. You must love and understand dogs.'

She snorted. 'I'm the old woman that would rather have a picture window than a dog!' she said sharply.

From her post at the picture window the old woman

watched the children. It didn't work – her strategy.
The children were following her instructions literally.
She could see them at times running and playing
around the wood-lot, then they would make brief
marches across the empty field again, but always they
kept looking back over their shoulders, and always
they hurried back to the copse. Maybe they're over
doing it, she thought to herself. They're trying too
hard and making it artificial. Maybe they should do
what they did this morning – just keep calling his
name. She turned as if she had half a mind to go out
to them, but then she turned back to the window. 'I've
a notion,' she muttered to herself, 'that he's still more
afraid of women than of men – she with her broom
for a puppy!'

Late in the afternoon the exhausted, disappointed
children gave up. They could not manufacture any
more play. There was no laughter in them; they were
too close to tears. Once more as they trudged away
across the field towards the house, the boy sent out
his last hopeless call: 'Candy, Candy.' Then they
walked on. They did not look back. They'd given up.

'Something went badly wrong,' the old woman at
the window muttered as she watched the children. 'I
guessed wrong.' Suddenly her eyes flicked back to the
copse – a slight movement there had caught her eye.
There he stood! On a little knoll outside the copse,
for the first time in plain sight. He had one leg drawn
up. He stood staring mutely after the children.

'Call now, call now,' the woman at the window
urged under her breath. The children trudged on. Still
the dog stood there. Suddenly he turned his head. The
woman turned her eyes to look where the dog was
looking. When she looked back the little dog had
disappeared; something in the copse must have scared
him. 'That did it,' the woman bitterly told herself.

The children came into the house.

The girl and boy walked into the room and stood before their grandmother in utter desolation. 'He didn't come,' George managed to say. 'He's gone, I guess.'

'No,' their grandmother said. 'He isn't. I saw him again just before you came into the house, so he's there . . . But don't worry, you've done enough. I suspect he didn't intend to follow you anyway, just watch you out of sight. But you two can start right now being happy again. I talked to Captain Carlson on the phone. And do you know what he told me? You're each to get a brand-new bicycle for all you've done!'

They couldn't believe her. It was too sudden a full-ness in the emptiness of their disappointment and defeat. Their grandmother carefully had to repeat every word the captain had said.

The girl had a momentary conscience-stricken scare at the thought of going to the strange man for the reward when they didn't have the little dog. 'Maybe if we do it once more – just walk from the copse across the field to the house . . .'

'No,' her grandmother decided. 'No, you're over-tired and you've done enough. And maybe it isn't even good – him moving about so much with that bad leg. No, you go right upstairs now and lie down and rest, and talk about bicycles until your father comes to take you home.' She smiled at them fondly.

When the children had gone upstairs the old woman once more went to the telephone, but this time to warn the captain that the children were coming for their reward. 'I seemed to have to do it that way, they were so beaten and they'd worked so hard all day,' she apologized. She explained that the little dog had briefly emerged from the copse once more. 'But

I'm afraid he has no feeling of belonging to them any more. I guess he belongs wholly to you now. So there's only one thing left – food! So this is my plan. Tonight I'm once more setting out my food pan, but tonight I'm going to be cruel and mean about it. The pan's just going to smell of food – oh, maybe a dribble in it to sharpen and tease his hunger. But I suspect that's how he lived the past year – scrounging food from house to house. So if he gets nothing here, he might keep going on to the next house, he might even go as far as your house – and then if you'd have some good food set out . . .'

The captain eagerly explained that he had already arranged for a big pan of mince to be set at his kitchen door.

'Ah,' she said, 'between the two of us – a little brains and a lot of love . . . But I'm sorry about the children coming and my just arranging it like that for you, but they were so beaten.'

'It's fine about the children, and you are wonderful,' he said.

The children had come and gone. Abashed and excited, standing before the captain lying on the couch, they'd been only too eager to be away. They had gone off with their father, dancing with excitement all around him, both talking excitedly to him at the same time. 'Two bicycles cost much more than fifty dollars, don't they, Dad?' George had demanded. 'But we're just to go to the store and pick them out, and we didn't even find Candy. He's rich, isn't he, Dad?'

'Mine's going to be all red,' Catherine had announced. 'Bright red, with just a tiny thin white line . . .'

'Mine's going to be a racer.' George had tried to outdo his sister.

'We'll see, we'll see,' the distracted father had kept saying over and over.

In the house, Martha, the cleaning woman, was making preparations to leave for the night. 'Did you set out the mince?' the captain shouted after her.

She answered from the kitchen door. 'It's all set, just as you wanted it, and I'm leaving the door open. I'll try to be back about ten in the morning.'

That was last sound until night came after an endless twilight. The window at the couch was open. The crutches were set where the man could reach them. Evening insect sounds shrilled outside the window, but then all sounds slowly drifted into night stillness. The hours wore on. Now, slowly as the hours had gone, it was deep night, and still the man on the couch kept vigil. The phone at his elbow, after a short preliminary ping, shrilled through the silent house.

It was the old woman. 'He's been here, and he's gone – three footprints in the smooth wet dirt around my food pan. Now we can only hope he's on his way to you.'

'Goodness, have you stayed up all this time?'

'I had to see it through, but now I'm really going to bed. You'll let me know the first thing in the morning, won't you?'

The night was edging towards morning and now the moon was out. The little dog sat on a knoll under an apple tree, the highest point in a high field. He sat tense. He could not see it, but the teasing, luring, lovely odours of meat came to him again in the field, carried to him on a small night breeze. Across the field rose the tall white house among the pine trees. The food odours came from that house, the house that had been his house.

Now the moon drifted from behind clouds; moonlight glinted along the blue roof against the stark green of the pine trees. It glinted momentarily on the yellow straw broom still hanging in the pine tree. It was as if it gave him courage, the silly, helpless broom hanging there so high. He stole from under the night shadows of the apple tree; he edged a little closer to the house, but then he sat again.

An hour later he had edged into the yard. He carefully kept to the shadows of the outhouses. At last he neared the garage, the last shadowed building between him and the pan with food in the bare, moonlit yard. He tensed, ready for the last three-legged hobble across the yard, and the snatching of the first hungry mouthful of food. But as he came around the corner of the garage, there in full view stood a broom! A broom stood against the house directly behind the pan of food. The desperation of his hunger oozed out of him. He backed away into the shadows and hobbled away.

Under the apple tree in the high field he stopped to rest. His tortured body, after his long journey, could take no more. He trembled with weakness. He was weak with a terrible hunger, and across the field the food odours came lilting again on the night breezes, and the broom swayed in the pine tree. Suddenly the little dog lifted his head. Out of his tight throat broke the hopeless sing-song of his misery. And into it he sang all his helplessness and hopelessness and loneliness, and all the misery of brooms and hunger and desertion, and the cruelty of men.

In the house the big man lifted his head, propped himself up. He lay listening to the little dog's wail, as if by the very intensity of his listening he could force the little dog to come closer. But the miserable thin howl came no closer. 'He doesn't dare; he wants to come but doesn't dare,' the man said softly.

He lunged up from his couch, grabbed the crutches. His big body wasn't used to them. He made several clumsy tries, but at last he had the crutches under him. He swung himself awkwardly out to the kitchen and the wide-open kitchen door. He stood in the moonlit doorway, peering everywhere. In the field under the apple tree the dog had fallen silent at the first sight of him.

The man on the crutches waited. Then he tentatively tried it. 'Candy,' he called. 'Candy, Candy, Candy.'

He listened after each call, but the night lay silent. 'Maybe,' he muttered to himself, 'if I go inside and leave it to the mince.' He turned. And then he saw the broom the cleaning woman had left standing against the house. Suddenly he was in a towering rage. 'That woman!' He muttered savage, violent things; he swung himself towards the broom and grabbed it. Somehow he balanced himself on one crutch and with fierce, wrathful strength swung the broom far from him. It twisted and spiralled, and spun away into a tree. There it clung. The man muttered things at it and violently swung himself into the house, but behind him he left the door wide open.

In the high field under the shadows of the apple tree the little dog had seen it all. Had seen the big man suddenly appear on crutches. Had listened to the big man calling him for the first time by his name. He had listened and he had tested it, but he had not dared to yield to it and obey. He had not dared to believe it. But then he had seen the man lunge at the broom and hurl it twisting through the air. The broom still hung there in the tree, but now it was all over; the great, good man was gone. But the food stood there, and the door stood open.

The little dog came forward a few tentative steps. He sat again. But as he sat an impelling urge came in him to wave his tail, and he got up again. Once more he advanced across the field. Once more he approached the house, but he seemed to have to approach it by the same old hidden cautious way he had approached it before. At last he sat in the shadows of the outhouses again. He was gathering his last courage. But as he sat in the shadows there came a stumping in the house, and then the captain, awkwardly balancing himself on one crutch, appeared in the doorway once more.

The big man carried a pan, and from the pan came new warm meat odours. Lovely, heavenly warm odours came lilting across the yard. Still the dog sat secret and unseen in the shadows. Now the captain set down the pan with new warm food in the kitchen, a foot or two beyond the open door. Then the man straightened up, and then came his order clearly across the silent yard. 'Candy! Hurry home, Candy. Candy, you come home!' And then stumping clumsily the man disappeared in the house.

The warm food stood in the kitchen just beyond the moonlit door. The food stood there, the order of the great good man still stood there: 'Hurry home, Candy. Candy, you come home!'

The little dog left the shadows. But he couldn't go straight. He still warily had to circle the buildings on his slow three legs. But every circle brought him closer to the open kitchen door. And now between him and the open door lay only the naked, moonlit yard. And the brooms hung in the pine trees.

In the shadows of the garage the little dog sat fighting his last timid hesitation, sat fighting with the compelling odours of the good, warm food, sat testing the last spoken order of the great good man. 'Hurry home, Candy. Candy, you come home!' Once more the urge came to him to wag and wave his tail.

The little dog stood up; the little dog had started to obey. And in a moment he would walk across the open yard and through an open door. And then he would be in. Then he would not merely have a pan of food, he'd have a home, he'd have a name, he'd have a love for a great, good man. A love for a man that would grow and grow in a great, good life with the man. A love so huge, and so complete and so eternal, the little dog would hardly be able to encompass it in his one little timid heart.

Hurry home, Candy. Oh, little dog, why don't you go now? Why don't you hurry home?

The little dog stepped out of the shadows, and on three legs the little dog went home.

The Hunting
of Wilberforce Pike

MOLLY LEFEBURE

Wilberforce Pike is a cruel, red-whiskered, cat-thief, who snatches unsuspecting felines to be made into fur coats. Oliver Simpkin, a previously sheltered pet, is one of Pike's first captives, but the fearless Power Station gang comes to his rescue and saves his skin. He joins them in the mysterious cat underworld and swears to bring revenge on the villain Pike and his equally sinister wife. And so the mad chase begins . . .

This is an extremely funny book, with a strong, adventurous story-line, for readers of ten upwards.

'A refreshing and hilarious story with some unforgettable characters.'
Eastern Daily Mail